The Game in the Past

The Game in the Past

John Zeugner

RESOURCE *Publications* · Eugene, Oregon

THE GAME IN THE PAST

Resource Publications
An Imprint of Wipf and Stock Publishers
199 W. 8th Ave., Suite 3
Eugene, OR 97401

www.wipfandstock.com

PAPERBACK ISBN: 978-1-5326-0520-8
HARDCOVER ISBN: 978-1-5326-0522-2
EBOOK ISBN: 978-1-5326-0521-5

Manufactured in the U.S.A.

in memory of
Hiromu Magofuku

Thinking is an attempt to apprehend Reality by catching it in a conceptual net, and a net is able to serve its purpose in virtue of having a texture which leaves gaps between the meshes. It is this open texture which gives a net its fling. If the net were made, not of an open network, but of a tightly woven cloth, the material would be too heavy to allow a net made of it to be effectively extensive. But the price of having a texture which makes it possible to catch something in the net's meshes is the inevitability that something else will slip out of the net through the gaps.

—Arnold J. Toynbee, *Reconsiderations, Volume 12* of
A Study of History.

Contents

Part I, Guade's Recruitment, 1979

Historical insight Professor David Moran believed was the end product of diligent, extensive preparation. Only after you had been through and been through and been through the data did the connections begin to emerge.

"Historical linkage—I abjure the term, causality—surfaces only in so far as you rescue the elements of the past from their natural habitat at the bottom of the sea." Moran had pontificated the sentence more than once to that pasty and malproportioned collection of graduate students who were forced each year to take the department's seminar on historical methods. "If those elements breathe, it is because you have carried air to them. To pump life into the past you may have to yield sustenance, breath, in the present. The endeavor requires commitment, dedication, monastic discipline, and certain fascination for the inert—a willingness to sacrifice living now in order to discover what it might have been like to refuse that decision in the past."

All well and good. Repeated earnestly, automatically. No need to check its validity. He believed it once as he composed the phrases, rehearsed them for the dutiful graduate students. The repetition was entirely appropriate and Moran discovered that as the sentiment meant less and less to him, his mouthing of it became more and more convincing. In the early days he had logged up his monastic time. A book on Clarence Gauss, the U.S. Ambassador to China during World War II, had come of it, and tenure and a certain admission to the lower echelons of the mildly revisionist historians of the Cold War. His name turned up more and more regularly at the conclaves of diplomatic history. A modest national reputation had led, through a unique conjunction of recommendations, to the lecturing assignment in Japan. And the apex of the assignment was, apparently, the summer convocation of Cold War historiographers at a posh hotel on a mountain top overlooking Kyoto. Moran and seventeen Japanese historians had been summoned to comment on the most recent papers of the profession's most ascendant star. At thirty-four Graham Guade, a full professor for four years, had published six books detailing with exquisite density of footnotes in five languages, the interplay of strategy that controlled and throttled U.S. diplomacy from 1942 to 1954.

Guade wore a hearing aid, an oversize beige object clamped to the back of his right ear, a shiny clear plastic line plunging, apparently, into the center of his brain. Moran thought, for a while, he saw fluid from Clio traveling instantly into that categorizing mind. The aid made Guade anomalous. He looked younger than his age, had a rather fit body which might have been, save for a little padding, called athletic. His motions were controlled but incessant. He cast off waves of energy, constant motion that signaled aliveness, and somehow ferocity. And yet the aid enveloped the energy in an image of neurasthenia—as if the young Vulcan had traded in his club foot for a beige tumor behind his right ear. He wore light flannel plaid shirts entirely appropriate to his Western, athletic image. Moran imagined the Japanese saw him as the quintessential American—open, bluff, vigorous, an intellectual cowboy quickly propping up the dominos of their beloved stereotypes.

Each morning he dazzled them by reading a dense, brilliantly documented paper on the American concept of a defensive perimeter in Asia, capping that effort on the last day with fifty pages on the collapse of perimeter strategy in Korea in June, 1950. As always the Japanese made no comment. They took notes and nodded, having no appetite, no sympathy for verbal combat. Guade appeared puzzled by the silence, kept prodding his audience demanding an end to stillness. It fell to Moran to keep the discussion period from collapsing as thoroughly as the strategy Guade had analyzed. Their watched conversation veered quickly out of criticism of the paper. Moran, as always, was awed by the scholarship, overwhelmed by the logic. Instead, he and Guade talked about the importance of certain documents, the accessibility of others, and finally speculated on any American troop withdrawals from Korea. Would the U.S. intervene, for example, if the North Koreans came down across the demilitarized zone?

"When you get to hypotheticals and predictions I guess you can say the discussion has run out of substance," Guade laughed, refusing to answer the question.

Suddenly a Japanese at the far end of the table began speaking British-accented English. "Isn't the real problem than no one in the State Department in Washington, or in the U.S. knew very much about Korea in the period after World War II? There was no one who had any knowledge of the peninsula. Isn't that the real problem?"

Guade seemed delighted the Japanese had spoken; his reply was slow in coming, measured, apparently thoughtful. "I believe you are right. Acheson certainly had almost no feel for the Korean situation. It is a very telling point."

Moran wondered if the Japanese understood that idiom.

"I'm trying to think who might have had Korean expertise," Guade continued.

"When did Hornbeck leave the department?" Moran volunteered, "And what about Atcheson, George Atcheson?" The two names Moran could summon up from the Department's Far Eastern Desk.

The Japanese professor, amazingly, rose quickly to the challenge. "Hornbeck knew nothing of Korea. He was a so called 'China hand.'"

"And Atcheson," Guade continued, "was killed in a plane crash in 1947."

"Well, I suppose that settles it," Moran said. "It seems the less the U.S. knows about an area, the more likely it is to intervene there."

"Maybe intervene is the wrong word," Guade said, smiling.

"We could try decimate," Moran answered, smiling his best Japanese smile, a signal that whatever you're doing is not what I want.

Guade looked annoyed. Silence fell over the group and the chairman asked for further questions. When there were none, Guade suggested an early break for luncheon.

"So you think America is the scourge of the world?" Guade said to Moran in the bar afterwards.

"You don't?" Moran answered.

"There have been lamentable incidents," Guade went on, eyes bantering over the top of a Gin and Tonic.

"You know you can't get decent tonic water in Japan," Moran said. "For some reason Schweppes hasn't gotten here yet in 1979."

"I see," Guade continued, "you wish to overlook my defense of the U.S., flood over it with your superior knowledge of Japan."

"My knowledge of Japan . . . it's true I've listened to too many arguments over whether we vaporized 140 thousand or 200 thousand folks in less than six seconds. Hiroshima's Peace Park is a good place to test out whether *decimate* is too strong a term. But my true Japanese expertise concerns Gin—it's a bargain here. Nobody drinks it but visiting professors and, of course, Brits in Kobe."

"We agree to disagree," Guade said. "I see you have adopted Japanese tactics. Now you can smile and cock your head, indicating that you know I'm an idiot who must, nonetheless, be indulged."

"Precisely, only my smile indicates you deserve to die," Moran said.

"Well, anyway, one of them," Guade motioned to the Japanese who had clustered at two far tables, "actually said something today. I must be making progress. I appreciate you're coming up with some names."

"In graduate school I did a paper on Hornbeck and Atcheson. Their world view or some such. I ended up thinking Atcheson was a Communist. So you see we aren't so far apart politically."

"Absurd," Guade countered.

"Our agreement, or my judgment on Atcheson?"

"Both."

"Have you read Atcheson's China dispatches?"

"No. But his anti-communism when he came here to Japan on the Commission after the war was well known—even embarrassing."

"A cover, like my smile."

"Ridiculous."

"Well, read the China dispatches and then tell me what you think. Though you'll have a bitch of a time finding U.S. government documents here. I don't think *Foreign Relations of the U.S.* series exists in Kansai."

"They certainly do at Doshisha," Guade said.

"Well, they certainly don't at the national universities."

"Tell you what. Come to Tokyo next month for the seminar and we can argue about Atcheson," Guade said paternally.

"What seminar?"

"A kind of reunion—the original proponent of the perimeter theory, including Liv Wells."

"The Undersecretary for Marshall?"

"Byrnes," Guade corrected him, smiling.

"Touché."

"I'll get you invited. You can even do a colloquium if you like."

"I don't like."

"Well, just a private discussion then."

"A history lesson?"

"Of course! Atcheson was no traitor," Guade said, with just enough earnestness to stop the conversation— banter scattered.

2.

Moran actually had the China FRUS volumes with him in Japan. He wanted to write a follow up article on some recent students of the China Foreign Service Officers and there was grant money to air freight the FRUS volumes to Osaka. For the next week he worked over Atcheson's dispatches, once again, cutting new notecards. He knew Guade would find his own volumes, knew that Guade would be rigorous and thorough and energetic in marshalling his evidence. Moran understood well enough that preconceptions inevitably shaped data, so he tried to make the case for Atcheson's naiveté or anti-Communism, or simply a failure understand Mao and Chou. But he became certain there was no other way to explain Atcheson's long dispatches explicating Marxian theory, or his agonized employment of that theory to justify new moves on the part of Stalin or Mao. Why should a counselor or attaché be so obsessed with the theory of Communism?

Guade could, doubtless would, point to changes of tone. Early Atcheson cheered the Communists on, but by 1945 he had begun to call the reforms a veneer for something else, begun to sound the anti-Russian incantation that characterized his post war work in Tokyo. But all ideologues risked disenchantment and all traitors understood the use of cover, didn't they?

At the opening of the seminar sponsored by the American Center, Guade took Moran aside, to a corridor adjacent to the small lecture hall. "I've looked at the dispatches," he said.

"So have I, again."

"We should talk."

"Aha! Is it a certain sense of contrition I hear in your tone?"

"More than that. We need to discuss several things. I've been to the states since Kyoto."

"To the states and back?"

"Yes."

"And you've discovered Atcheson was really Alger Hiss?"

"I've a series of questions for you and a couple of envelopes. Let's try to get some *yaki tori* after the panel. Meet me right here as soon as we're through, can you?"

During the discussion Moran kept turning over in his mind Guade's tone and insistence, as if he had taken on a certain respect for Moran, or at least seriousness toward him. Could it be had re-read Moran's book on Gauss? That seemed unlikely. More probably Guade was hooked on an anti-Communist persuasion and glad to find new candidates for pillory. Moran was convinced of his own accusations against Atcheson, but equally convinced that such information was irrelevant, nothing more than a game one played with the data. But it occurred to him that providing such game data to someone like Guade who took the enterprise with the utmost seriousness was rather like tossing an ember into a pool of gasoline—an image which seemed appropriate to the glowing brazier of the *yaki tori* place they found. They took two stools at one end of the twenty that formed a semi-circle around the open hearth. Moran ordered beer but Guade refused to drink.

"The dispatches are interesting in that they display a man trying to apply dialectic theory to actual occurrences. It's not simply a matter of reporting favorably on Mao or the Communists in Yenan."

"Exactly," Moran said.

The chef, in a sort of sawed-off, brilliantly-colored robe, dispensed charcoaled delicacies from off a long-handled wooden paddle. The Japanese on the other stools kept up a cascade of laughter and conversation. Already most of them had a red band around their eyes, which signaled intoxication. Moran always felt buoyant in such places. He siphoned off the incomprehensible exhilaration around him, drank furiously, and pointed to whatever he wanted cooked on the grill. He knew enough of the names to get favorites like chicken (*tori*), shrimp (*ebi*), and squid (*iika*). Guade was not interested in the ambiance of the place. He talked incessantly, made references to certain dates, certain dispatches, displaying, as always, total command, total recall, of the material, but Moran ceased to follow the exposition. He was settling over the edge of his stool, dribbling down the sides as Sapporo Ebisu beer worked its wondrous relaxation. Why was Guade talking so?

"With Davies and Service and to a certain extent Vincent, you catch enthusiasm for what seems to be a democratic regime run by Mao, but Atcheson is never interested in that. When Stalin suspends the Comintern Atcheson spends two pages explaining how this can be done under Marxist theory. I mean who was reading such a dispatch? Who could have cared? Alone among the China officers he seems mesmerized with dogma, theory, dialectics. It's astonishing."

"Of course. Of course," Moran answered. "I never thought McCarthy had a shred of evidence against Service or Davies or Vincent, but against Atcheson, I thought there was a case and he never tried it."

"Atcheson dies in August, 1947. McCarthy didn't start ranting 'till early 1950."

"I know that. I guess you need living enemies. But Atcheson would have been the perfect target. He never even got mentioned."

"Hurley accused him and all of them in 1945."

"Hurley doesn't count. Who cares about one bitter, Indian-bonneted Ambassador for chrissakes?"

"There's more to Atcheson," Guade hunched over, as if full of intrigue and revelation.

But Moran, after three large bottles of Ebisu, watched him from a perch about thirty feet overhead. Down below it

9

seemed the Japanese squealed in abandon. A waitress moved on the outside of the semi-circle distributing more *sake* or beer to the increasingly noisy patrons.

"Essentially the dispatches raise significant questions and you have to answer why would somebody be writing such things? Why would somebody want to display control of Marxian theory as an interpretive prism of events in China?"

"I give up. Why?" Moran laughed. He liked the slow, mechanical way the chef brought the paddle to the grill and then slowly swung it toward the crowd revealing something to eat on the end. The paddle stopped at the correct orderer.

"I formed three hypotheses—"

"Just three?"

Guade looked carefully at Moran's focusing eyes. "Yes, just three: One, he'd done some reading, maybe brushed up against Marxism, and was practicing to test his own comprehension of the schemes—bored in China. I know Foreign Service Officers do that, a kind of detachment from the impact of their own statements. Writing in the void and so to make some order you tend to test out theories that structure what you're living in."

"A kind of interpretation verging on apologia," Moran said. He contemplated dipping his grilled onion slice in a side dish of raw beaten egg.

"Admittedly so, number two is that he was, after all, what Hurley thought he was, a Communist, committed, in a cell someplace and he merely analyzed the world, especially Russian actions, as a Communist might. Or three, he was an apprentice Communist filing dispatches to his mentor in the movement."

"Ah, conspiracy!" Moran said, chomping on the mucusy onion. "I like that. Commies were everywhere you know.

But you don't exactly sound as skeptical as I imagined you would."

"The data go elsewhere," Guade said. "So you have to know more about him. What his background was, and who he reported to."

"Gauss?" Moran asked.

"You know the answer to that," Guade answered.

"Yes, indeed. Not Gauss. Blessed Clarence for once gets some benefit from being ignored."

"Since I had to go back to D.C. anyway, I checked the archives and asked to pull his 123 file from State Department records."

Moran has spent almost two hours going through Gauss's 123 file. 123's were usually fairly tame collections of innocuous personal documents—birthday greetings, letters from old friends concerning department business, sometimes photographs, occasionally a copy of a letter of recommendation, sometimes, if you were lucky, some diary entries that for one reason or another didn't end up in the personal papers; often enough, only travel vouchers.

"But," Guade went on, "it wasn't there."

"Someone had pulled it?"

"No. It was simply gone, disappeared. He had no 123 file. But that was unacceptable, so I asked to see the invoice of accessioned boxes when the stuff came over from State in 1957. And it wasn't on the list. Ten packages of Foreign Service stuff, nine 123 files, none for Atcheson. It never came over. Lots of other Atcheson stuff, but not that. So I went over to State and said I wanted a trace on the Atcheson material before 1957. Where was it and who handled it?"

"All because of my joke in Kyoto?"

"You weren't joking," Guade said levelly. "Now follow this, pay attention and stop drinking your beer. In 1947,

September of 1947, all of the Atcheson holdings went to an Air Force base in California, as part of the investigation of the plane crash that killed him. The holdings were requisitioned by a Lt. Kimball in charge of the Flight Accident Investigation, and the transfer was authorized by the Undersecretary, after consultation with the White House."

"And they wouldn't let you into the Air Force base?"

"Not funny. I haven't been yet. I was more interested in why the investigation of a plane crash, the technical investigation of what it was that brought the plane down, required a review of <u>all</u> of Atcheson's records."

"Because he had a long history of fiddling with explosives?"

"The plane ran out of gas, ditched off Hawaii. No explosion."

"Because Kimball was his brother-in-law? Because Atcheson had top secret clearance and any accidental death requires thorough investigation including the possibility of assassination?"

"Hardly," Guade said, and then stopped abruptly.

Moran, who had gotten used to Guade's recitation in the same way he had gotten used to inexplicable Japanese noises around him, was jolted by the silence.

"Wasn't that an interpreter at the seminar?" Guade nodded in the direction of a Japanese toward the middle of the semi-circle. The fellow was wearing oversize tortoise shell glasses.

"Where?"

"Ten over, with the draft beer."

"No."

"He wasn't up front. He was doing the simultaneous stuff from a booth in the back, behind you. I'm sure of it.

You couldn't see him unless you turned around, but I had to watch him all the time."

"Maybe he's a killer, a Japanese *ninja*."

"Not funny. It's just interesting he should turn up here, don't you think? Maybe I should pass you the envelopes now."

"Jesus, I am certainly sorry I said a word about Atcheson. In fact, I take it back. He was as American as apple pie, with *shoyu*."

"What?"

"Soy sauce."

"I see," Guade said staring now at the apparent interpreter, whose eyes were surrounded by the tell-tale red band. The interpreter suddenly looked back, smiled, half-waved. Guade waved back. Moran could see him assessing the Japanese, reaching an innocent verdict and dismissing him to return to Atcheson's greater conspiracy.

"We need much more data," Guade said, "much greater access. But that might take years, would be equivalent to doing a biography, so I've decided to take a short cut and focus directly on the death. Why should the Air Force want to have a passenger's background to determine the technical failures of a B-17 flight? Why would consultation with the White House be necessary? And what did the final accident report conclude? The Times is rather muddled. It says the plane ran out of gas and ditched about 40 miles off Oahu in very rough seas. But the pilot reported having eight hours of fuel when he left Kwajalein, more than enough for the four-hour flight. One of the technicians guessed that the number 2 engine which had been replaced en route in Guam had turned out to be a 'gas eater' but that surely would have been clear by Kwajalein. So a plane with plenty of fuel runs out of gas, ditches. There are four survivors. Atcheson is never found. Never found. Six bodies are recovered. Four aren't. One of them presumably was Atcheson. The Times says the Coast Guard Cutter Hermes approached one body, but it sank out of sight in the last seconds before it could be pulled aboard."

"It sounds like an accident to me."

"Undoubtedly was, but why have all of Atcheson's papers go to Norton Air Force base in California?"

Moran had stopped listening. He watched as the waitress opened a large electronic console in the far corner of the restaurant's tent over the grill. She undid a small microphone and slowly carried it to a patron sitting near the middle of the semi-circle. "Jesus," Moran said, "now we get the singing."

Guade suddenly took a half swallow of his beer. "No we don't. I haven't told you the half of it yet. Come on. We'll go back to my hotel."

Moran signaled the waitress, paid her twelve thousand yen. Guade forgot about the dinner check, but insisted on splitting the cab fare back to the Hilton.

"Atcheson drowned, slipped into the Pacific. No body. None. Ever."

Moran stood a bit woozily in the gold lame light of the Hilton lobby, while Guade showed his hotel booklet and got his key. This shining world surpassed, Moran surmised, the cramped quarters of his business hotel in Shinjuku.

"He had one son, and I understand his wife came for sea burial ceremonies in Hawaii, but erected a monument in Denver. That's an interesting problem, isn't it—putting up a tombstone for a body not there?" Guade continued in the elevator, Moran watching his own widening grin in the circular mirror mounted on the back wall. "So in terms of removal Atcheson's death was about as antiseptic as you could ask for."

The corridor was grey-white and carpeted in grey-pink, spongy thickness, but Moran was delighted to find out

Guade's room was scarcely larger than his own in Shinjuku. There was one substantial difference. Guade's bureau had a miniature bar on top of it, a rack of choice liquors in tiny bottles, and there was a refrigerator.

Moran unhesitatingly opened a tiny scotch bottle.

"I pay for that in the morning," Guade said, irritated.

"I'll deduct from the dinner tab," Moran answered.

Guade sat on the bed, which doubled as a couch. Moran sank into a narrow straight-backed wicker chair opposite.

"Atcheson's death—" Guade said.

"Look," Moran interrupted, "I only made a suggestion about Atcheson. What's the point in getting so riled up over it? I don't think it makes any real difference. What would happen if you could show Atcheson was Mata Hari? Who'd care? And what would it prove historically?"

"You can't make evaluations before the story is clear, can you?" Guade answered. "Why judge the data at the outset? You assemble the data and then decide. You simply can't judge the sources at the outset."

"As good a time as any," More said. The T.V. seemed better than his Shinjuku version which was suspended about 18 inches from his bed.

"I want you to do something for me," Guade said.

"Only if you pay your tab."

Guade stared straight at the scotch bottle, then took a five thousand yen note from his wallet. "Are we even? Those cost 1,800 yen."

"More than even," Moran answered, taking the note.

"I want you to ask a question tomorrow. I want you to ask Wells a question. About Atcheson. Ask him why the Air Force wanted to see Atcheson's papers as part of the Flight Accident Investigation."

"And he'll know?"

"He authorized the transfer, as often as not, from '43 on Atcheson reported to him."

"And Wells being here was also an accident?"

"You must have known it," Guade said. "You must have foreseen it. That's the best part. You set me up!"

"Don't be absurd."

"You'll ask the question?"

"Why not? It's a bland enough question."

Part II, Moran's Distraction

When Moran left he carried a large manila envelope, which Guade explained would reveal the other half of it he had promised. By exiting from the rear of the Hilton, using a floor below the lobby, it was possible to walk directly into a subway entrance of the Chiyoda line. Then by taking two enormous down escalators and walking the full length of the platform and then three escalators up you could get to the Marunouchi line without ever surfacing. The Chiyoda line platform was sparklingly new—greenish polished cement and tiles, and, surprisingly, without many passengers waiting for the next train. Walking the platform Moran decided was like stepping into a long horizontal urinal. You waited for the rushing water that came as the train arrived and in the meanwhile only your steps echoed in the gleaming porcelain tube.

He decided to stick the manila envelope inside his coat jacket. He clamped his arm against it. Safe. Unsnatchable. All of which, he knew, was absurd. Scotch-topped paranoia was contagious. For a while Moran imagined he was followed. On the first up escalator he slowly turned around and was disappointed to see only two school girls at the bottom.

Moran remembered a Guade-like fellow in graduate school who insisted one night in reciting for him all the outrageous accusations of the 1884 Presidential election, as if Moran would be equally mesmerized, indeed enchanted by Cleveland's and Blaine's taunts. Moran knew well enough the obsessional turn of mind such students had, but he was surprised that Guade, the polished scholar shared the disposition. Only the tiniest, jesting nudge had sent him charging into the documents, had tossed him against bureaucracy's doors. Might it have been possible Guade was the first U.S. historian ever to demand to see accession lists at State? Who else would have thought of it? Only, Moran decided, the most diligent of conspiracy hunters, that is, those without choices beyond the ferreting life. And what did the ferreting life yield as benefit? Only its own obsession and commitment—it's terrific determination to discover something in the void of the past at the expense of the present? Only its ferocity of determination to find something out that ultimately became an interpretive mirage anyway? Still there was Guade's enviable energy, focus, stellar unconsciousness. Who knew what those implements might yield?

Moran took the local to Shinjuku san-chome. He exited through the basement of Isetan Department Store, and then, in a sudden lurch of sentiment turned right rather than left and started walking toward the main Shinjuku Station, the entertainment district. His business hotel was quite the other direction, a choice, he decided a thousand, more likely several thousand, Japanese business men made every evening. Japanese movies and television shows were filled with the adventures of peasants from Kyushu or Hokkaido who couldn't keep away from the attractions surrounding Shinjuku Station.

This main entertainment district, the *kabukicho*, was a grid of narrow streets, closed to most cars, and suddenly on all sides by bars, night clubs, game parlors, pachinko parlors, strip shows, discos, tiny eating places (with six or eight stools at the counter), basement coffee houses and on top floor, lounges. Before every building tuxedoed barkers poured out beckonings in the scarlet and orange-filled sky. Neon pulsated; the clouds overhead contained apparently, fluorescent lights. Reams of wandering Japanese, men with arms around each other, propping each other up in order to vomit, chic couples in the latest gear—army fatigues, string dresses, wide lapel suits, elegant frost white blouses, white patent leather shoes. And spreading charcoal fumes. Wine stink. Sake scents. Boiling water humidity bathing the area. Lurid posters and mechanical neon signs, and withal, a constant babble in another language. Moran could only pick out phrases. He was better used to the slurring of the dialect in Osaka. There appeared to be a greater precision of pronunciation in Tokyo, less emotive signaling in the phrases, yet more hostility in the muted tones.

Moran stopped first at a ramen stand and ordered another bottle of beer. Then, bolstered, he headed back out into the throngs. He oriented himself by keeping an eye on the enormous billboard atop a building that ran the full length of the block, advertising a sado-masochist show. When the rant of the barkers became more insistent and the neon grew more brilliantly orange, Moran knew he had entered the roadway of so called "love hotels" and "Turko baths". And then a young, apparently Japanese fellow, in a slightly stained double breasted tuxedo was standing in front of him speaking insistently into Moran's face—about ten inches, it seemed, from his nose. Was it English?

"Good time, eh? Very good time in here. And not so expensive. Good time, eh? Eh?"

Moran instinctively drew back, but the fellow pressed in. His breath, like that of lots of Japanese, smelled foul. "Good time?" Moran queried attempting to slow the pressure.

"Yes. So. So. Very good time. I fix it for you. I fix it for you. Come on in. Come in now!"

"How much?" Moran asked, back stepping further.

"Very inexpensive. Come on, I'll show you. He grabbed Moran's left arm. Moran felt the envelope shifting. He clamped it harder to his side and went along with the fellow.

At first Moran thought they were going upstairs, but instead they passed beyond the stairway and with shoes still on came into a thickly carpeted lobby. There appeared to be a hotel registration desk.

"What is this?" Moran said, suddenly steadying fighting down the beer and scotch."

"Turko. You know Turko? Don't you want a bath? I think you do. I fix it for you. I find you a nice one speaking English. You'll like this one. Don't you want to?"

"Why not?"

"Yes! Yes!"

"How much?"

"You pay me two thousand yen. I set it up. Then you pay what she says. Okay?"

"Okay," Moran said. He set the envelope on the counter top, got out his wallet and took two one thousand yen notes out, self-consciously keeping the extent of his holdings from general view. Moran felt strangely in control, as if he were designing the sequence of events. He had heard about Turkish baths, but the direct action possible in Shinjuku seemed liberating. And the scotch/beer empowering. If he were in charge, what could go wrong? Japan always left him always in charge if totally dependent. Japan was the safest spot on earth. And if he perished here, who would be upset anyway? Only this fellow whose unlined face and features like those Moran imagined American Indians must have possessed for the Pilgrims, bespoke only eagerness to please. No simply taking the money and running. He brought back a slender, short woman who was, Moran estimated, about thirty years old. She carried a red plastic shopping basket and a large sponge. She smiled and her one-piece jump suit with the sleeves and pants cut off at the highest joints reminded Moran suddenly of car hops in Florida. Was she on roller skates?

No, indeed, although she fairly glided upstairs, Moran following, the tuxedoed fellow smiling and bowing with each of Moran's backward glances. About half way up the stairs Moran saw the envelope still on the Registry counter. He stopped, abruptly wheeled and bounded back down. He jumped the last five steps, vaulted to the desk and snatched the envelope up. Suddenly he felt absurdly foolish. The woman on the stairs smiled at him and waved him to come back up. Moran looked at the tuxedoed fellow, then held the envelope up. "Life insurance policies," Moran shouted.

He went quickly back up the stairs. She led him to one of about fifteen doors opening off a long corridor. They came into a small six by ten foot room with a narrow massage table against one wall. There was a second room opening off the first. This contained a tiny, rather shallow bath tub. She motioned for him to take off his clothes. As he took off each garment she folded each with exaggerated carefulness, fitting each into the basket. When he was naked she handed him a traditional Japanese towel about nine by twenty inches of thin almost transparent white cotton. Then she indicated he should sit on the massage table. He put the towel across his loins. She stroked the hair on his chest, treating it with wonder and, he sensed, a rehearsed satisfaction. After she had tucked the basket on the floor under the table, she turned back to him and in rapid-fire Japanese said something that sounded like, "Sucki nee mahn en."

"Eh?" Moran answered, trying to ferret out the meaning from the sounds.

"Sucki nee mahn en," she repeated quickly, business-like, implacable.

Moran knew his numbers, "nee mahn en," meant 20,000 yen, more than he had. "Ni mahn yen, desuka?" Moran asked to confirm the amount and to get more time to figure out what "sucki" might mean. He considered whether she meant it in Japanese or English, or did it mean the same in both languages?

"Hai, so desu," she quickly confirmed the amount.

"Takai," Moran answered, drawing out the last syllable, a device in Osaka that indicated the price was too expensive.

She appeared not to follow that evaluation.

Moran felt acutely vulnerable. The door to the corridor had been left open and it seemed the room was designedly cold. Chilled down. Moran shift his thin towel protection. He remembered clearly enough that in Japan you didn't haggle. You didn't bargain. Crude counter-offers were considered insulting. The door had been left open he decided to settle such insults definitively.

"Ni mahn yen?" he asked again.

"So desu," she answered automatically with, he figured, a tinge of impatience.

"I don't have it," Moran said in slow, hyper-articulated English.

She smiled at him.

"I'm sorry," Moran went on.

"Sucki nee mahn en?" she said again, sighing.

"Iiya," Moran answered, "gomen . . . gomen," apologizing in his pidgeon Japanese.

"Okay," she said, "okay. Take bath."

She does speak some English, Moran thought. She drew a tub, scrubbed his back, insisted he wash his own genitals. Then after wiping him dry with the thin towel, she indicated he should lie down on his stomach on the table.

He eased onto the chilly vinyl and she leaned in over his right ear and whispered, "Skoshi mo?"

Moran did not have even an inkling what she was saying. "Eh?" he answered

In a breathy, exciting way she leaned in again, hot scallops of minted breath coming over his neck and ear, "Skoshi mo?"

When he didn't answer she abruptly flipped the wet towel lengthwise down his back, over his buttocks, and started pounding the backs of his legs, then his shoulders. After a few minutes of this she leaped up on the table and began walking on his back in a way that signaled, it seemed, disgust with him. The door was still open. There could be no defense in this situation, Moran thought. He remembered that it was mostly Koreans who ran the Turkos. Koreans hardly succumbed to Japanese civility and pacifism. He imagined he had been set up. In another moment the enforcers would be in the room and with truncheons extract full payment.

She jumped down and said again, "Skoshi mo?"

"Wakarimasen," Moran answered. "I don't understand."

"Okay. Time up," she said. She put the basket up on the table and indicated he should get down and dressed. She stood quietly by as he got into his clothes and then when he slipped his coat back on she held out her crossed palms.

"How much?"

"Two thousand yen," she answered in apparently perfect English. "Downstairs you may have tea or beer. Which would you like?"

"Beer."

She preceded down the steps, guided him to a western style couch and then brought him a mug of draft beer.

"Thanks," Moran said.

"Arigatoh," she answered and went swiftly back through the doors from which thirty minutes before she had appeared.

A disaster Moran thought but at least his worst fears had been avoided. He was still intact. Perhaps she felt the same way. An absurdity of miscommunication. He would have to find out what "Skoshi mo" meant, or would he? He might savor the suggestiveness of it. Suppose he found it only meant "a hot night," or "tomorrow is a holiday, thank God." He quickly finished the beer, sensitive that a foreigner in the main lounge might inhibit business. When Moran got to the double glass doors and saw the tuxedoed barker on the street rushing up to new recruits, he suddenly remembered, "Jesus! The envelope!"

He glanced around. No one was in the lounge. He quickly went upstairs. He heard laughter from behind closed doors. But his door, as always, was open. He checked the basket, but the envelope wasn't there. Nor was it on the massage table, or beneath the mattress, or in the bathroom. Not behind the rattan stool in the bath. Moran slumped against the frame doorway, he remembered carrying the envelope upstairs, remembered setting down some place, but where? He systematically examined the room again, knelt and examined the bath floor. Two absurdities, he thought, a double unfulfilment.

He went back downstairs, waited by the desk but no one came out. "Hello" Moran said strongly. "Onegai," he said requesting help. "Onegai!"

No response. As he started to look over the top of the registry, he heard the door open behind him. She came back out.

"My envelope," Moran said, pantomiming its shape. "Kaban, kind of—" he said recalling the word for briefcase. "Envelope. Where is it? Doko desuka?"

She smiled, went upstairs. Moran moved to the foot of the stairs. Soon enough she brought the envelope back down to him.

"Where did you find it?"

She smiled and walked quickly back through the door.

The tuxedoed barker let Moran out. "Good time, eh?" he said, his eyes dancing in phony delight.

"Terrific time," Moran answered, "the best ever." He clamped the envelope against his side under his left arm.

On the walk back to his hotel, once away from the heaviest crowds near the *kabukicho*, Moran opened the envelope. It contained three smaller white envelopes. In two of them he found wads of lined blank school notebook paper. In the third envelope there was only a pair of brown nylon socks with nifty little clocks stitched in the sides.

2.

C. Livingston Wells embodied his name, Moran decided. Immaculately suited in material that seemed softer than his jowls, more neatly trimmed than the spare silver hair tucked behind his ears, Wells sat stiffly behind a long white Formica table. To his right were Guade and two Japanese professors. Wells wore cufflinks, apparently translucent white discs joined by silver chains. He had a rather beefy face, but narrow shoulders suggesting a kind of elegant thinness. The face wasn't quite right, perhaps a tinge too red. Either too much adulation has brought a permanent blush, Moran felt, or else the old fellow is a tippler. But his eyes contained none of the tell-tale, yellow-clay tone Moran found in alcoholics.

Evidently there were more enthusiasts for the Cold War in Tokyo than in Kyoto. The circular lecture hall was crowded. Media types lined the walls. Who would have thought the collapse of the perimeter defense theory in June, 1950 would have stirred so many? Was Wells something of a hero in Japan? Did they think he was still connected with the government?

Guade led off the panel with six minutes of sharp comments demonstration how each federal bureaucracy viewed the Asia defense line differently in the spring of 1950. Internal contradiction, then, seemed to account for the speedy collapse of the doctrine, Guade asserted. The two Japanese colleagues also spoke about six minutes and Moran studied Wells rather than absorbing the headphone translation. Finally both the Japanese and then Guade asked Wells for his comments.

"A lot of this is ancient history splendidly resurrected by Professor Guade. I certainly have no substantive revision of his remarks. But I suppose I should say that in a bureaucracy, and especially at that time, lots of posturing, lots of position papers get generated—especially during slack times—that were never very seriously considered, even by their authors. Oh, they were assented to, duly stamped, logged, but always considered a kind of window dressing. Speculative exercises. Since crucial committees with authority to act seldom committed themselves in writing. They didn't have time or they found it, rightfully enough, binding in a way they wished to avoid. So I suppose admirable as Professor Guade's account is, it may be miss-focused, or concerned with policy declarations, rather than policy itself."

Guade said jocularly, 'I'd like to see your substantive revision, if that is your non-substantive reaction."

"Perhaps I've wandered out over my head. I don't mean to suggest people didn't believe their papers, but rather their belief was a double nature, what you Japanese so skillfully identify as *tatemae*, the official explanation, the public sentiment, versus *honne*, the real, private, accurate assessment. It is *tatemae* that these places, USIS or rather ICA (must keep up to date with our acronyms, mustn't we!) these libraries are interested only in public information exchange. The *honne* is, of course, the desire to present America as favorably as possible, to win allegiances to American life and concepts of government, and so on, and so on. Some *honne* is part of *tatemae*, of course, but I suppose a great deal of *tatemae* is not ever *honne*. I must say, too, that at the time of the invasion I was off the Allied Control Council in Japan. In point of fact I was on leave, since my wife was recovering from her first operation."

Wells stopped talking, waited for comments or questions. But there was a typical silence in the lecture room. To cover Wells said, "Beyond all this laudable historical analysis I feel it incumbent to say something about the real world we live in today in 1979. For the present the U.S. is still terribly committed to the defense of South Korea and should the attack come in the form it took in June, 1950 surely the U.S. would intervene to defend its ally. Somebody ought to say that publicly and unequivocally."

This pledge of support by a retired official seemed, Moran noted, to inspire the audience. There followed a series of elaborate statements in Japanese from the floor. Invariably each ended with the justifying question: "Would you comment on that?" Clearly there was no sentiment for question and answer, only the mutual airing of variant positions in the endless quest for further information.

Wells smiled through all these briefings avuncularly. Apparently he followed the Japanese discussion directly for he had conspicuously left his ear phone on the table top. The responses he made were soothing and appropriate, agreeing with several points, omitting controversial ones and after each juncture of evaluation introducing an appealing anecdote.

After forty minutes of such one-way colloquy, Moran decided it was time to shatter the immense saturninity. He was the first foreigner with a question. When his arm went up, Guade instantly designated him the next speaker, and the ICA attendant rushed to give him the hand microphone. Moran watched as Guade leaned in on the table to study Wells' answer.

"Mr. Undersecretary," Moran started, "can you tell us why the Air Force requested all of George Atcheson's personal and diplomatic correspondence when it investigated his plane accident?"

"A very specific question," Wells said, smiling, "unlike some of the more cosmic efforts heretofore. Atcheson? Atcheson? Do you mean Dean Acheson, whose plane so far as I knew never had an accident?"

"No sir, I mean George Atcheson, with a 'T' who was a senior member of the Control Commission here in Tokyo, as well as a former China hand, and Ambassador to Japan, I'm sure you remember. He was lost in a plane accident in August, 1947."

"1947," Wells said, "A long time ago, and your question is?"

"Why did the Air Force want to see all his files, just to investigate the plane crash, the ditching of the B-17 he was taking back to the states?"

"I'm not sure I could answer that. Have you asked the Air Force?"

"No, sir. Is it routine to send out the total file of a Foreign Service officer lost in the field."

"Are you sure it happened?"

"Absolutely."

"Well, it surprises me. There must have been good reason. Perhaps you should contact the Air Force. George Atcheson? George, did you say?"

"Yes, sir."

"Well, there was nothing special about that flight that I can remember."

"Except, of course, it was special for Atcheson," Moran said.

"Indeed. Indeed. I'm at a loss, I'm sorry. Someone at State should be able to help you.

"Thank you," Moran sat down. Guade had been jotting notes the whole time.

Very skillful, Moran thought. It was impossible to tell whether Wells was only feigning or was truly bewildered. Moran did notice that Wells could not stop glancing at him even while fielding other Japanese comments. Bewildered then, or upset, or both—Moran couldn't decide.

In fifteen more minutes, however, something of a decision formed, for Wells, having dutifully commented on a rambling speech about the impact economically of the Korean War, suddenly returned to Atcheson. "It occurs to me concerning a previous question from the gentleman over there, that I do remember George Atcheson and his tragedy, now that you remind me of it. And he was highly respected

in Japan, and it was a stupid accident. And I believe he was—
I mean his body was never found, isn't that correct?"

"Yes," Moran said, "but I was asking about the transfer
of his files to Norton Air Force base in California."

"Yes, yes, I quite remember your question," Wells said,
evidently warming to the task. "And about such a transfer, it
did occur, didn't it? You might ask in the State Department,
Garret Weaver, if he's still there. I remember he handled the
files at about that time. When was it again?"

"August, 1947."

"Yes, in the summer of 1947, in the late summer. And
you say all the files were shipped to where?"

"Norton Air Force base in California."

"All of them?"

"Yes."

"Well, well, you should try Weaver on that one. Yes, I
would try Weaver. I'm sorry I can't be more help."

In five more minutes Guade ended the discussion and as
the hall emptied, joined Moran near the simultaneous translation booth in the back. At first Moran thought he should
immediately apologize for losing whatever had been in the
envelope, but as Guade approached him a certain wariness
took hold. To his own amazement, either out of guilt or perhaps fear, he held back and let Guade direct the conversation.

Guade merely motioned him away from the booth toward the metal stacks of the library proper adjacent to the
lecture room.

"Thanks," Guade said. "He wasn't exactly forthcoming,
was he?"

"Well, you have Weaver's name to pursue."

"Hmmn," Guade said, "Didn't it strike you a bit odd
he pretended not to remember Atcheson. But Atcheson reported to him."

"He recovered on that."

"Precisely. Deliberate recovery. You go through that stuff I gave you?"

"No. Not yet. To tell the truth I nearly passed out on the subway. When I got back to the hotel I simply folded up."

"Okay. Okay. No rush, I suppose. He signed the transfer order, Weaver didn't."

"Who is Weaver?"

"Never heard of him," Guade suddenly looked around. There was a youngish Japanese fellow in a lightly billowy suit nearby. He seemed to be examining some of the oversize books. "Look, I've got to go to lunch. Why don't you call me tonight, or we could get together later, after you've gone through the stuff. You will get to it, won't you?"

"I'm not sure it's worth my time. I started you out on this, and it's turned out to be a little more than the lark, the joke, I intended."

"It's no joke, not yet anyway," Guade said. He rocked back, adjusted something in his hearing aid. "Where's the stuff now?"

"In my hotel room."

"In the open?"

"In my bag."

"Hmmn, and you haven't looked at it?"

"No. I didn't get the chance," Moran could truthfully say.

"Well, call me later, will you?"

"Okay. I'll try to get to it this afternoon." The hotel story would cover, Moran realized. If when he got back only socks and torn school paper were in the envelope, the transfer could have occurred any time during his absence. "But there is a bit of a problem."

"What?" Guade said, all attention.

"You can't get into business hotels till after 4:00 p.m. You have to leave by 10:00 a.m. and you can't come back before 4:00."

"Well, why don't you check on Weaver, using whatever they have here?"

"No. I'm going to Asakusa to sight see, or maybe to Meiji Shrine, or maybe both. But I'll call you tonight. I'll get to it as soon as I get back to the hotel."

"Okay, okay. Call any time after 9:30 or so."

"Well, it may be later than that."

"Any time. Just call."

"Were you pleased with his answer to your question?"

"Not pleased. Confused. I'll pursue it at lunch. Call me tonight."

"Yes. Yes," Moran answered, a bit irritated at Guade's constant directives.

Outside the building he caught a cab to Shimbashi station. He decided Asakusa was too far away, on the other edge of the city, and so settled for Meiji Shrine, even though that meant riding the JNR loop line which was always crowded and somewhat confusing. At the station Moran ate a bowl of noodles, a far cry from Guade's doubtless elegant luncheon with Wells. On the other hand, Wells might not enjoy it. A consummate fencing match, Guade anxiously dropping bits of information and Wells easing past them, foisting them off on the mysterious Weaver. Even the name seemed right— Weaver. Moran made his way upstairs to the JNR line. For some reason there were fewer English signs on that line but Moran managed to get to Harajuku, the stop for Meiji. He followed the crowds through the extraordinarily wide gravel walkways. He was careful to step over the timber in the doorway to the shrine. It was either irreligious or unlucky to step on the sill, he remembered, and Moran felt neither and both. When he got to the inner court of the shrine, he was approached by an elderly Japanese gentleman who was, remarkably, unkempt and not recently shaven.

"I must beg your acquaintance and indulgence," the old man said, "for my English is all inadequate, but I need to practice."

Moran stiffened for the inevitable questions. The afternoon suddenly seemed sultry. The breeze died away and the open spaces seemed occupied by heavy, humid air that would have to be penetrated for exit.

"You perhaps have looked into these cuts and nicks on these august timbers."

Moran noticed them only because the old man pointed them out.

"They were made by hurled coins. At new Years, our most celebration time thousands of we Japanese come here to make an offering to the shrine. The ones in the back have to throw their offerings. Hence these marks. Isn't it interesting to you?"

Moran knew the old man had memorized the speech and he wondered if the fellow knew what he was saying, or had only gotten a native speaker to coach him on the sounds. "Yes, very interesting," Moran said, moving away from the interior court.

The old man followed. "How long have you been in Japan?"

"Not very long," Moran answered.

"Why did you come?"

"I teach here, or rather in Kansai."

"When will you leave Japan?" The old man went on. So the questions as well as the speech were memorized.

"Not for a while," Moran said, consciously speeding up his pace on the gravel.

The old man hastened to keep up. "What did you expect Japan to be like. Do you like we Japanese?"

"Ah yes. Yes." Moran said, "Very much. You are very civilized."

"Thank you. I must leave now. I have enjoyed our English conversation. But my English is so poor. I must harder and harder at it. Thank you, again."

"Thank you for the information," Moran said to the old man who was already in a deep bow. The old man stood up, reached into his pocket and held out his card for Moran to take.

"My *meishi*," the old man said, "you may call on me any time."

Moran was familiar with this custom. He should now proffer his own *meishi* but that would lead, he was certain to more, endless English conversations. "Thank you, I'm sorry I don't have a card to give you."

"That is correct and satisfactory to me." The old man bowed again and back stepped, bowing. Involuntarily Moran returned the effort. In the still air he and the old man continued this back stepping and bowing until Moran felt his shoe bang into the top edge of the sill to the shrine.

3.

At 9:30 p.m. Moran called Guade's room, but there was no answer. He called again at 10:00, and at 10:20. Still no answer. At 10:40 he called the front desk to ask if there were message for him from Guade.

"Professor Guade has checked out from the hotel," the clerk said in slow, hyper-articulated English.

"Checked out? You mean left?"

"So. So, so," the clerk answered.

"He is no longer at the hotel, is that it?"

"Yes. He has gone."

"Where did he go?"

"Pardon?"

"Where did he leave for?"

"For?"

"Never mind. Did he leave a message for me, Professor David Moran. Perhaps an envelope?"

"Just a minute, please."

Moran watched the blinking neon of the station area through his window. The business hotel room was barely five by ten feet.

"Did you say, Molan?"

"Yes, Molan. Molan," Moran answered emphasizing the Japanese miss-pronunciation.

"There is a phone number on the paper marked for Professor Molan. Would you like it?"

"Yes, please."

When the clerk gave it to him Moran thought he recognized the exchange—an area near Shinjuku station. Guade must have found cheaper accommodations. But a European woman answered with a simple "Hello."

"Is Professor Guade there?" Moran asked. Could Guade have somebody in Tokyo, a liaison? The idea seemed incongruent to Moran. What would they do together? Crank microfilm readers?

"Is this Moran *sensei*?" the woman's voice gave a strange mockery to the Japanese addition of teacher or learned one to Moran's name.

"Yes."

"Well, Graham isn't here, but I'm supposed to tell you that he's gone off to Shikoku with Liv Wells for four or five days. They're taking a ship on the Inland Sea and going to some famous park in Shikoku."

"Ritsurin?" Moran said.

"Yes, I believe that's it."

"Did Professor Guade leave any instructions for me?"

"Instructions?"

"Directives, assignments, things he wanted done?" Moran slowed down his speech; it seemed the woman was not a native speaker.

"No. Graham said he was having trouble communicating with the hotel clerk. He was in a rush. I think they took the 7:00 p.m. *shinkansen*. So he called me."

"I see," Moran said.

"I do translation for him, for his research—every time he comes to Tokyo."

Every time, Moran thought.

"But he didn't leave any instructions. Maybe he'll call you from Kobe, although he's on a tight schedule. They wanted to catch the last ferry tonight."

"I see. Well, okay, then. I guess I'll talk to him when I talk to him. I go back to Osaka tomorrow."

"I'm sure he'll get in touch. Is there anything else, in case I talk to him before you do?"

Moran debated a while, then decided it was providential she turned up as a shield as well as deliverer of bad news. "You might mention to him, if you do talk to him, that there's been an accident with the envelope he gave me. It doesn't seem to have anything but blank sheets in it. So I really can't evaluate blank sheets."

"An accident?"

"Well, my poor choice of word. Maybe not an accident, maybe a theft or just a mistake or something. He might have given me the wrong envelope. He'll know what I'm talking about."

"And I should not tell him there's been an accident?"

"Yes. Just tell him I can't evaluate the information because I don't have it. The envelope had only blank pages torn out from a notebook. Nothing was written on the pages. Nothing."

"Okay, I'll tell him, if that's what you want."

"Yes, thank you. I'm sorry to bother you so late."

"No bother. I never go to bed before two or three in the morning."

"Well, goodbye. Thanks again."

"Don't mention it. I'm glad to be Graham's messenger, especially to such a distinguished sounding voice."

Hmmn, Moran smiled, wondered, then thought better of it. "Well, goodbye," he said.

With any luck she would break the news to Guade, who might then be so angered as never to contact Moran again— a prospect entirely appealing to him. The neatest way out.

Moran watched the show "11 p.m." sometimes referred to as "The Men's Hour." On good nights the pornography was vivid and startling, but now he had to make do watching a leggy young woman who stripped to a G string and writhed on a black Naugahyde couch. The couch was covered with some kind of oil—Moran hoped it was Baby oil—and soon enough the model was oiled and glistening in the splendid definition of Japanese television. A panel of overweight Japanese men drank glasses of Suntory whisky and made low comments and guffaws concerning her performance. Even though he had put two 100 yen coins into the T.V. Moran turned it off at 11:45. He chained the door shut and lay back on the soft bed. He conjured pairs in his mind before dropping off to sleep: Guade and Wells, Atcheson and the Pacific

Ocean; Moran and the expensive masseuse. He wondered if he should try the socks on. The thought pleased him. Without turning on the light he fumbled around for the envelope in his bag, pulled out the interior envelope and removed the socks. They were way too small—doubtless her own?

In the morning he managed to catch the 9:12 *hikari shinkansen*, the fastest bullet train back to Osaka. He sat on the right and watched for Mt. Fuji. In the five trips to Tokyo he had always seen the peak and that was considered good luck, but although he strained all the way to Nagoya, this time the heavy, grey atmosphere was too thick

He took the Midosuji line from Shin Osaka station to Senri Chuo, then caught a cab to his apartment in Yamada. Violating his own rules, he actually looked through his lectures on the Cold War to be given Monday and Tuesday at the university. He was more than prepared since most of his students did not understand what he was saying. He stood before them speaking sounds, and after a while he joined them in wondering what he was saying, wondering if they understood even a preposition he muttered. He decided the best historians merely babble and you listen only as they did when foraging the past, for what you already knew. He would have to try that sentiment on the historical methods seminar, if he ever returned to the U.S. He had been long enough in Japan for everywhere else to stop existing. He stopped his subscription to the English language newspaper. He self-sealed the envelope of Japan. The green mountains perpetually available through train and bus windows were more than enough to look at, or on the other side glimpses of the dark green sea. For diversion there was the endless array of faces framed in equal mounds of black hair. The people cascade never stopped—so profuse that after a while you didn't need, didn't want, anyone to share it with.

4.

On Monday and Tuesday mornings he walked to Senri Chuo, caught the 8:40 bus to the university and delivered as slowly as he possibly could his treasured perceptions of the U.S. and the Soviet Union from 1945 to 1954. There never were any questions. The classroom was narrow, but long, easily housing his sixty-five students from the Faculties of Technology and Pharmacology. He stood up front by a laboratory demonstration table and occasionally held up a printed summary of his remarks, pointing to key portions, crucial phrases. Before, and afterwards, Moran sat in the smelly, dank common room, drank luke-warm green tea and tried to make linguistic jokes with some of his Japanese colleagues. He wondered if their English was any better than his students'. It was certainly better than his own Japanese.

Moran did not teach on Wednesdays. Usually he slept late on the tatami mats of his eight by ten foot living/dining/sleeping room. Then he walked down to the nearest market to purchase fresh pastries, wondrous imitation French and Danish varieties. The shopkeeper set aside three for him. He read a bit till noon, or answered mail, or sketched out alternative outlines for his book on the Cold War and by 1:00 p.m. was on the Hankyu line to downtown Osaka, most probably to see a double feature at the Dai Mai Chika, a cheap theater that specialized in older American films. Translations in Japanese appear along the right edge of the screen—side titles. Clint Eastwood was a favorite of Osaka audiences, as well as all films with cartoon-like violence. The side titles were disconcerting. It was peculiar to hear the audience laugh before the joke was spoken in English on the screen. They have an advantage even watching our films, Moran thought. The theater was near the American Center

Library. On particularly disorienting or lonely days Moran ended up in the library reading its collection of magazines and newspapers until closing time at 9:30 p.m.

This Wednesday, after a double bill of Eastwood, Moran decided to pursue Atcheson through whatever holdings the Center library had. Since the China recognition the library had stocked a series of monographs on U.S.-Chinese relations. Atcheson was good for a mention in several of them.

Atcheson was the son of a doctor. All good revolutionaries spring from bourgeois origins, the long western tradition of the mock aristocrat leading the rabble to new dignity aptly borne out here, Moran decided. Atcheson trained at Berkeley then became a journalist after World War I and then a stint in China. Was he radicalized by the sobering experience of reporting objective conditions of the masses? One could impose easily enough, Moran discovered, the prevailing pattern of American radicals on Atcheson's life. Well-to-do origins, extensive liberal education, broadening, sensitizing experience in professions that led per force to exposure to the exploited underclass: newspaper reporting, or prison instruction, or missionary field work, or a series of part-time jobs in that permanent part-time segment of American labor.

But it was too neat. Moran knew he brought too much to the data—too much baggage from the John Reed model of American radicalism. So Moran began to toy with a more plausible, less theoretical explanation. Perhaps Atcheson experienced a disillusionment with the nobility of his easy childhood, the automatic acquisitions of the American good life. Didn't Atcheson's conscious life (whatever that meant) begin in China. Wouldn't his education start there too? Everything before that was programmatic, expected, unconscious. Was that it? The inert Atcheson stirred only in a foreign culture and only after peering deeply into a window of butchery. That might be it. It sounded good, anyway. What a profusion of alternatives the enormity of China's disintegration must have tossed up to the would-be revolutionary. Suffering on a scale as to be visible even to the American doctor's son who doubtless imagined meals and clean linen, clean carpets, and clear windows were, after all, the permanent structure of the world, not the grimy work of other human beings. The esthete in the slaughterhouse, was that it? As an organizing principle the model appealed to Moran, for reasons he knew enough not to dwell on.

And besides, if one were looking for a transforming experience Atcheson clearly had one in December of 1934. The twenty-nine year old Consul had to travel out from Tsintin to identify the mutilated bodies of a missionary couple. In particular the State Department seemed determined to allay suspicions of sexual assault. The most graphic inquiries came over the cable and Atcheson was ordered to establish or refute allegations he might not have imagined. The five year old daughter of the slain couple apparently was being safely held in a village near the murder. She would have to be retrieved, as would the bodies, then tagged and sent to the coast for shipboard return via Hawaii, unless air transport could be arranged. And the precise mutilation would have to be detailed.

What might this nasty task reveal to Atcheson? The power of conviction? The absurdity of idealism? The intransigence of the Supreme Being whose "work" the couple so loyally had been doing? The ferocity of the world?

The village belonged, Moran decided to the Communists. Could it have been Chou En-lai himself who ushered the young American through this little test? Moran imagined that Atcheson was steered through the open-skied village toward a last hut in which rested two pine coffins. And Chou waited by the first one. "I admire their spirit," he might have said, "their dedication. Your country sends us only their best and we emulate them, as best we can. Then this sort of thing happens to remind us how much stronger they, and you, are than we are. Do you believe it?"

Atcheson might have answered except that Chou turned back the loose plank of the larger coffin and the Reverend Michael Foresmeer's headless body came into view, the neatly severed neck topped by a towel now a tired maroon color and sealed with waxed paper.

At the American Center Moran was sitting in a hypermodern white chrome and canvas chair, with a clear view to the water cooler and three video tape monitors. Two of the televisions were playing soundless tapes of Richard Nixon at some news conference, the third carried what appeared to be an interview with an American woman Moran didn't recognize. Nixon appeared embarrassed and angry and grinning; the woman appeared languid, tranquil, vaguely sensual. The images formed an appropriate background, Moran decided, for Chou's lesson, whatever that might have been.

Atcheson caught himself in mid vomit, swallowed down the inner accumulations and finally whispered. "How can I make an identification?"

Chou pointed to another towel, grey and maroon stained by the corpse's elbow.

"You don't mean . . . "

"I do, unfortunately. The devil who did this insisted that the physical possession of head alone insured their sanctity from dread westernization. We could not reason with them. Killed them outright to get this sad remnant back. A good word in English, remnant—says so much. Should I continue?"

"Yes."

There was a creaking sound that Atcheson would never forget, an adhesive pulling apart as the towel came away, flaking off bits of dried blood. "You must not imagine this is our norm. The residue of a dying society defies human classification and tosses up hideous exploiters. But you should remember that alone among our enemies—Japanese or Chinese—we have not recruited such butchers. We offer reform or rejection; we do not offer employment to such scum. When it's necessary we kill them to rid them from us. Do you understand?"

Atcheson noticed for the first time the odd stench and melon scent that might have transported him in other circumstances. Corpses should not smell this aromatic, he decided, as defense against the quick shift of space and sense occasioned by the wide open, horrified eyes of Reverend Foresmeer.

"He saw," Chou said, closing the lids of the eyes, or rather trying to close them, but, amazingly, they resisted the gentle stroking Chou undertook. "He saw the China passing away and it smote him dead, did it not, Mr. Atcheson? But you will see the China being born, here in this place which sheltered his daughter from the scum to which he surrendered. And new China extracted justice from these butchers. His invoked cross was feeble enough, I might note without rancor and in sadness. But we shall fulfill him. Can you go again for Reverend's wife?" Chou asked, easing back the planks topping the second coffin.

Atcheson did not respond. Like Moran he watched the soundless tape and attempted to mouth out the message being delivered and waited to be shown what had happened.

Two butcheries, Moran decided, does not generate reason, even if Chou himself were the explicator. The doctor's son felt other compulsions. What were they?

On the other hand, random violence needed rational orienting, needed to slip into familiar nets of familiar orderings, and dialectic was wondrous in encompassing the explosive extremes. Chou could have shown him that. In the face of chaos one follows the most serene and fixed model at hand. And there was Chou not three feet away, explaining, and explaining, and explaining. He surely knew that Atcheson hardly cared who did the killing, but was desperate to be told why the killing was meaningful. He saw immediately Atcheson's obsession not to blame but to dismiss through some reasoned consideration. Dismiss, excuse, transcend. Atcheson needed to find a way to write his report without shifting continuously through crazy sorrow, official distancing, mindless moralizing, and anxious commiseration. Writing his report hardly compensated for his disorientation.

Nixon slouched and scowled as the camera panned to his audience of interviewers, reporters on a promontory overlooking the sea. Then the tape backed up and Nixon slouched and scowled again. On the third monitor the American woman's wrist slowly, gracefully lifted her delicate finger displaying a ring made apparently of gold and jade, just as Atcheson untowelled the head of Reverend Foresmeer's wife. Delicate grey hairs clicked from dried blood coatings, snapping like the static in the jumping videotape images.

The rigors of dialectic, the laws of science, economics, historical movement grasped all this, made it jump, didn't it? Or at least Chou's elegant soft English provided adhesive for such separables. The towel flopped back and Atcheson saw directly into her brain through the eyeless left socket of her skull. At first he could not fathom it, the grey mound that seemed so recessed in her left eye. He understood it only when he scanned across the face and found in the towel edge near her right temple an extra eyeball streaming a blue grey phlegm-like substance.

"There was no sexual assault," Chou said easily, an absolution for the devils responsible. "Do you wish to verify that?"

Atcheson still stared at the eyeless socket. He had an overwhelming urge to stick his finger in, to test the texture of the grey matter, perhaps to taste it.

"We don't know how that happened," Chou said, "perhaps in the transport of the bodies here. Perhaps in the embalming. Perhaps somewhere else."

"Yes," Atcheson said, "somewhere else." He had trouble talking.

"Do you wish to verify there was no sexual abuse?"

"It won't be necessary," Atcheson said mechanically.

"It's done then," Chou answered. "You have been through quite enough."

Nixon waved to the reporters as he exited. The woman retracted her slim fingers, coiled her lithe hand. Moran watched the screens go to cool grey. And the Japanese who had checked out the tapes returned them to the gleaming white front desk. At 9:30 Moran walked back to Umeda station and took the local back to Yamada.

Part III, Turid's Moment

He heard his phone ringing from the front lobby by the mailboxes. He momentarily hesitated, then sprinted to his metal backdoor entrance on the first floor. Naturally the key didn't work easily. The caller would have to give up, he decided, but at length the door did swing back. Without taking off his shoes (evoking an immediate twinge of conscience he was amused to note) he lurched across the little genkan hallway especially created for shoe removal, into his kitchen and seized the phone.

"You are there!" she said.

Moran tried to fix the voice, clearly not Japanese. "Excuse me," he panted.

"Professor Moran?"

"Yes. Yes, what is it?"

"We talked in Tokyo. It's Turid. Do you remember? Graham's translator."

"Yes. I'm sorry. I was rushing to get the phone. I'm sorry. I didn't expect to hear your voice."

There was a long, strange pause. "I'm the one who's sorry."

Moran had a familiar empty, sinking feeling. "About what?" he asked.

"I have terrible news."

"You do?" A series of possible catastrophes turned over in Moran's mind. He imagined some Japanese bureaucrat actually concluded from the data at hand that she could be considered his closest relative and thereby trusted to deliver family tragedy. Bureaucrats were tireless in fashioning such constructs and getting *gaijin* to leave Japan, the real aim of such news.

"I have terrible news. . . Graham's dead."

"What!" Instantly Moran knew incredulity was the least appropriate response.

"Mr. Wells called me two hours ago. There was an accident on the ferry coming back. Graham fell overboard and apparently drowned or was killed by the propellers. He's dead. The body's in Kobe right now. Mr. Wells had to go on to the Philippines. He got the body to the Consul's office and then called me. He wanted me to call Graham's wife, Sanae, but I've never talked to her. Do you know her?"

"No. I've never met her either."

"I told Mr. Wells that. So I think the Consulate will make the call, but the Consul wants me to come to Kobe to sign forms and escort the body to the airport, I think. Does that make any sense? If Mrs. Guade doesn't come, she'll need an agent for Graham's body here. The Consul wants me to do it, but I don't think it's appropriate."

Appropriate, Moran thought.

"I want to come down, but I don't think I should be her agent. Do you?"

"I don't know. Maybe she will come."

"Why would she want to do that?"

"I don't know."

"I think you should call the Consul, Barry Ramden, if you would."

"Why?" Moran said, stiffening for no reason he could immediately understand.

"Well, if an agent has to be designated, the Consul needs to know that before they call Mrs. Guade."

"I don't quite follow all of this."

"I told them you might be willing, since you're a colleague of Graham's."

"Willing?"

"To be the agent. I'll come down of course and help out, but if you'd be the agent then Mrs. Guade wouldn't have to come over."

"Why does there have to be an agent?"

"To sign releases and certify condition of the body prior to transport. And some other things. I don't know, but I don't think I should be the one. I don't think Graham would want it. Mr. Wells should have done it, don't you think? But he had to go on to the Philippines, or somewhere. I wasn't listening very well. I can't believe Graham's dead. Maybe it didn't happen, is that possible? Maybe . . . Could you call the Consul?" She reeled off a number for Moran who wrote it down in neat fashion on the engagement calendar with its picture of the 48 waterfalls in Nabari. "I told him you'd be willing. He's expecting your call. I couldn't think of anyone else. I'll come down and help in every way I know."

Moran imagined the ways. He slumped down on the lone kitchen chair, "I'm afraid I don't follow all of this. The Consul is expecting me to call?"

"Yes. I'm sorry. You're the only one I could think of."

"What am I supposed to say to the fellow?"

"I'm sorry. I shouldn't have mentioned you, but to tell the truth, I can't quite believe what is going on. How can it be? Graham was a strong swimmer. Graham and I used to swim at Ise."

"What is the Consul's name?"

"Ramden, I think. Barry Ramden, or maybe Ramsden. I'm sorry. She needs to designate an agent and I shouldn't be the one. She shouldn't have to do that. He has a son."

Moran debated alternatives. "You take the next *hikari* to Shin Osaka station and call me. I'll call Ramsden or whatever his name is. And I suspect I'll end up calling Mrs. Guade. Jesus!"

But Ramden was not nearly so demanding. "All we need is for you to agree as her agent, if she wants it. I will take care of everything else. The Fulbright Commission has details of who to notify and how. We would never use a direct phone call to Mrs. Guade. There will be an intermediary—a minister or relative or somebody. I've heard she has a brother in Japan. Your task is to say yes, it's Professor Guade and yes, the body contained the following marcations upon loading for transport."

"Marcations?"

"Apparently Professor Guade could not avoid the propellers. His head is badly slashed," Ramden paused. "I'm afraid your job might be to persuade Mrs. Guade to keep the casket closed, for her sake."

"I see."

"Will you do it?"

"Wouldn't her brother be a more logical choice?"

"Our indication is that he never met Professor Guade. He'd not know him directly."

"He probably was at the wedding."

"Our indication is that he never met Prof. Guade. Will you come?"

"I guess so. Yes, of course."

"Good. The sooner the better. We need to get the body released for embalming. The Japanese paperwork is incredible. This is not the place to be born in, or to die in, if you're *gaijin*. Can you come immediately? The Embassy will pay the cab fare."

"All the way to Kobe?"

"Of course. I'd like to get the body on Pan Am flight #8 tomorrow afternoon, before the bureaucracy gets opened on Friday."

"What about tomorrow?"

"It's a national holiday. You didn't know?"

Moran didn't answer immediately. "You wish to short circuit the Japanese bureaucracy?"

"Short cut it. That's a better expression," Ramden said.

"I can't imagine getting away with that."

"We'll have the right people pulling for us, especially if you'll come right over."

"I'll guess I'll do it." He said a quick "sayonara" and then called Turid.

"It's just as well," she said, "there's no *shinkansen* this late. I could take a local down or a bus but it would be all night."

"All right, meet me at Shin Osaka at 11:00 a.m. No, at 10:00 a.m. I wish you hadn't got me into this."

"I'm sorry."

"How Japanese of you," Moran said suddenly angering.

"Well, I am sorry. But I'll make it up to you."

Moran turned that over in his mind and then said goodbye.

2.

The taxi took three hours and five minutes. Ramden was waiting at the guard house to the Consulate gate. A surprisingly young man, short, stocky, given to quick motions, he counted out eight thousand yen to the taxi drive, then added a thousand more. When the driver protested Ramden said, "Chippu, arigato gozaimashita." The driver accepted the tip. The first time Moran had seen that happen in Japan.

To make conversation as they walked to the larger stucco building, Moran said, "You're working late."

"So desu," Ramden replied, "it comes with the territory. I probably will take Monday off, unless you're planning to die then."

"I'll try to die in Kanto for you."

"I'd appreciate it. Have you looked at many corpses?"

"Only in caskets and after preparation—mine and theirs."

"Well, he's in a casket, but it's rather grim. I hope you don't have a sensitive stomach. I take it he wasn't a close friend of yours."

Moran wondered how Ramden had reached that conclusion but then said, "That bad, eh?"

"Indeed. Grim," Ramden repeated, "A real mess."

"Professor Guade was a fairly young man," Moran said, anxious to confirm distance between them.

"The youngest ever to do the Kyoto Summer Seminar lectures," Ramden added.

When they reached a larger backroom, Ramden motioned toward a stretcher table with a grey casket on it. The lid was off the casket, but Moran saw only a dark green vinyl body bag, neatly sealed. Ramden leaned in and slowly unzipped the bag.

"Most of the blood is dry. I sponged him off a good bit. But portions of the head aren't intact. Mr. Wells was fairly sure it's him, but he wanted verification."

"Wells did?"

"Yes. Are you ready? I should tell you an eye is more or less missing."

More or less was an accurate enough phrase Moran decided. Perhaps less than more. It was as if a meat cleaver had hacked two swift, deep blows through the left side of Guade's face. The top blow cracked away part of the temple, split the eye socket so that a trace of the eyeball's white lining and grey filmy substance rested at the edge of the nose, but the eye was absent, doubtless drained through the gash which opened pretty wide. The lower gash was neater, more surgical, following the grey pink of lips across the cheek and deep into the top of his neck. The lower cut could be pinched together, probably sown up, but the upper one was easily a finger width wide and perhaps three or four inches deep. It appeared portions of the brain had come out through the slash.

"Is it him?" Ramden asked.

Strangely Moran watched his left hand reach across Guade's face and feel for the hearing aid behind the right ear. It was still there. The features were Guade's but the hair seemed wrong—too dark. Moran finally decided only the wetness or the deadness accounted for the darkness.

"Yes, it's him," Moran said. "It was him."

Ramden steered Moran away from the casket, gently pushed him toward a red fiberglass chair, one of several along the wall near the door. Moran slumped down in the chair. He heard the zipper bag closed, watched the top of the grey casket come down into place.

"I don't think his wife should see that," Ramden said.

"Who are we to say?" Moran answered in irritation that surprised himself.

"It would serve no purpose," Ramden elaborated.

"I understand that you think it would serve no purpose. That might be a civil service response. I suppose you'd know." Moran continued letting more of his irritation out.

"I am sorry to have to use you for this," Ramden said.

"Will there be an autopsy?"

"If she wants one. It'll be done in the states, if I have anything to say about it. I don't imagine she'll want one."

"You're pretty good at imagining what other people want."

Ramden looked carefully at Moran, then seemed to draw a breath, as if shuffling stock responses to hostility. "It's necessary in this business and you get better at with each decade of dealing with situations like this." Ramden said slowly, emphasizing "each decade."

Moran stretched his legs out, arched a bit on the chair. His back had begun to ache. "How did you call Turid in Tokyo?"

"Mr. Wells suggested it and gave us the number."

"He knew her?"

"I don't know. I assume so."

"And she gave you my number?"

"Yes, I think so."

Moran sighed and said, "What now?"

"You can go home, or we can put you up if you want. Tomorrow after we've talked to Mrs. Guade, or if she calls us, we'll need you to authorize transport, authorize embalming, although we'll have to some embalming with or without authorization." Ramden shook his head indicating the smell was becoming serious. "After she's been notified, you could call Mrs. Guade and suggest to her that looking at Guade's body won't be, won't be—"

"Helpful?" Moran volunteered when Ramden struggled for the word.

"No. That's not it. It won't be reassuring to her. In the meanwhile before you leave, I want you to sign certain identification forms. Fortunately all his documents were with him in his travel bag."

"How did it happen, anyway?"

"Mr. Wells has left a statement. They were in a first class cabin and Professor Guade began feeling sea sick. Sometimes the Inland Sea can roll a bit, but not often. He decided to take some air from the rear deck."

"There's more than one deck?"

"No. Only one. Well, there's three but only one goes to the end of the stern. The other two are caged off. The main deck goes all the way to the anchor line. Apparently Professor Guade was examining the anchor line exit hole or whatever." Ramden waved his arms briefly to indicate he didn't know what actually it was called. "And he must have fallen right over the edge. When the anchor goes out, there's no lip there, nothing to hold you onboard."

"Right into the screws?"

"I would say so, wouldn't you?"

"Those were screw slashes all right. I used to visit springs in central Florida to watch manatees in the winter time."

"What?"

"Manatees, a kind of super seal or sea horse. Hideous, ugly creatures that come into the springs when the water got too cold outside. Long, pre-historic looking things, but their backs would be slashed up from propellers on motor boats in the bays or rivers before they got into the springs. Striated backs, they called 'em. Just like those cuts. Apparently manatees don't feel much pain."

"Oh, to be a manatee," Ramden said, following with a forced laugh.

"Did anyone see him fall?"

"The Kobe police are questioning the crew right now, but it seems pretty clear it was an accident. Are you thinking there might be something else?"

"No," Moran said. He imagined lots of historians might have sought something more than footnote vengeance on Guade, but no one ever accused historians of activism. "I'm sure it was an accident and I suppose Wells feels the same."

"Exactly," Ramden came over, sat on another chair next to Moran. "Of course the Kobe police wanted to talk with him, but he's on a lecture tour and was scheduled on Thai airlines for Manila, so they let him leave a statement behind."

"That must have taken some pull."

Ramden only smiled. How Japanese of him, Moran thought. "I understand," Ramden said. "It is a real loss to the history profession."

"He was talented, energetic, very good. But, on the other hand, nowadays historians are a dime a dozen."

Again Ramden smiled but more tentatively. "Do you want us to put you up?"

"Where?"

"Here, if you like, or downtown at a hotel. Probably the International. Rooms here would be more to your liking, I think."

"Okay. Here sounds good, but I'd like to do one thing more before we call it a night. I'd like to look at him once more, and I'd like to read Well's statement."

"Sure." Ramden quickly got up and pulled the casket cover back. He unzipped the bag. There was a peculiar old odor, rather like spoiled avocado, Moran decided.

The gashes were exactly as he remembered them, but this time Moran struggled to look at the non-gashed areas of Guade's head. The hair color was too dark, but the hair clearly felt wet. And when he pulled his fingertips away, the dark red stain on them showed what had darkened Guade's hair.

"Was the hearing aid in his ear when he got here?"

"Yes. I think so. No one here put it back on."

"Hmmn, isn't that a bit odd? You'd think that would be the first thing to go in a fall overboard." Moran wiggled the aid. It was tightly clamped around the ear, and even the audio wire plunged into the ear seemed rather taut, fixed. Guade heard his muse, then, at the very end—the skull resonating the slashing of the screw blades.

There was a dark blue bruise on the front of Guade's neck. Moran started to ask about it, and then some intuition stopped him, a swift sweet surrender to blossoming paranoia. For an instant even Ramden's cherubic face, his solicitous, ingratiating presence took on menace. Absurd, Moran thought and zipped up the bag himself. How distant Guade had become, a stack of manuscript papers to be turned through quickly for the one good illustrative quote. Research is distancing. The perfect preparation for sifting through the shards of this pre-eminent researcher.

"Enough grisly for one night," Moran said and they went back out of the storage room and on upstairs. Peculiar high-ceiling house for Japan. Fireplaces and rugs. Heavy, high furniture. The mansion of a German trader who settled in Kobe after World War I and then in the late 1920s sold to the Americans so he could return to the fatherland. The upstairs bedroom was airy, done in cherry paneling. Ramden put the folder with Well's statement on the mantel.

"You can give it back to me in the morning," Ramden said. "I suppose it's all right if you read it."

"The Kobe police have the original?"

"Yes, I think so. Mr. Wells made the copies himself downstairs."

"He must have worked fast."

"Well, he dictated to Miss Yamaguchi, who is very fast."

"I've never met a fast Japanese typist, a phenomenon indeed."

"She lived and worked in the states for ten years."

"Still, it's remarkable. She must have gotten this statement out in less than two hours. It's how long?"

"About three pages."

"Single or double spaced?"

"Single."

"Very, very impressive."

"Well, we can talk about it in the morning. I'll get you breakfast any time in the morning. Do you want a drink now?"

"No, thanks. I just need shaving equipment for the morning."

"Bathroom's all set up. V.I.P., since we're always ready for at least an Under Secretary. It's all yours."

"Indeed." Moran bowed and Ramden jerkily returned the bow, as if it were the most natural of exits.

Then Ramden added the standard Japanese sleep well phrase: "O yasumi nasai."

Moran heard it as both wishful and threatening.

3.

Swimming at Ise?

Moran's earliest encounter with Japan came through a National Geographic article on the wondrous women pearl divers at some place he thought was Ise. Naked from the waist up and below clothed only in soggy, wide G strings, these women soared through Moran's fifteen year old imagination. This surely was the Japan of one's dreams. And swimming with them was Turid—could that be? Also Guade without his hearing aid. Guade unhearing, knowing that he splashed only by the plumes of white-grey his hands and feet churned up. It was a bit improbable: the earnest microfilm reader had a Tokyo playmate?

More than improbable. Surely Guade would have vilified himself for that—all that time away from monographs or from document sifting, or perhaps they actually combined everything. She would have to be bright, and somewhat aggressive, Moran decided. Attractive, but used to fashioning reality so that it came out as she expected, indeed, as she desired. Tougher than Guade in ways Guade did not know existed. Guade the supreme naif, after all. Doubtless he only took up with her because it was expected, if not by his colleagues then by Turid herself. Moran imagined Guade was always living up to someone else's expectations, and Moran conceded Guade had more than enough energy for such carryings on.

On the other hand, she might have been no more than a helpmate. Additional footnote material, an access not to ecstasy, but only to clearer readings of the sources. A verb wheel for yet another language in Guade's voluminous citations.

But swimming at Ise bespoke revelry and affection at its tenderest—romance itself. Swimming at Ise. Did that mean chill hands and feet lolloping over the dry surface of Guade's orderly, ordering world? The helpmate could be prim, beady-faced and brusque—or the playmate blowzy and direct with occasional sidelong glances.

When they met at Shin Osaka station Moran decided she could not be subsumed in either category. Her manner, voice, conversation, had a detached, distracted turn, yet her appearance was easily within playmate parameters. Dark hair, rather gaunt frame, yet ample in a way that suggested a fuller life sometime before the sojourn in Japan. She wore brown corduroy jeans and a black, somewhat baggy turtleneck jersey. She carried a large brown plastic shopping bag labelled in silver letters, "Funky Babe." She had been standing opposite the reservation counter for Green Car tickets. They exchanged introductions. Moran even offered her one of his *meishi*. Then they went for coffee in a new shop called "Waterfall."

"You speak English easily enough," Moran said after the expensive coffees arrived. "Where are you from?"

"Norway," she answered looking around, and then appearing to forget what she had planned to say.

Moran, uneasy in this drift quickly rushed in with, "Where did you learn English so well?"

"Here," she said after a while, still glancing around in way that played on Moran's uneasiness. "I give a lot of Japanese lessons to American and British, if you can believe it. They're happier not learning from a westerner than they would be not learning from a Japanese."

"Perhaps it's less humiliating that way—not learning from your own kind."

"I'm not their kind. No way. And do they know it! They know it."

"I see," Moran said, resolving to try some silence to see where that might lead.

After a while she said, still looking around, "Have you viewed Graham?"

"Are you looking for, or waiting for someone?" Moran asked, irritated at her evident wish to be elsewhere.

"No. No, I don't think so, unless you have someone in mind, do you?"

"No," Moran answered. "I've . . . I've viewed Graham or what could be seen of him in a body bag."

She opened her eyes wider, fixed them on Moran, then away again. "They talked about mutilation," she said.

"Yes, slashes on his face from a propeller blade—or the ship's screws. One gash is very deep and hideous looking. But his hearing aid was still on."

"It's very hard to take off. He had the line bent in a funny way so that it locks into the ear."

"Well, it's there all right."

"And what now? Have you heard from his wife?"

"Her lawyer called this morning, early. I'm the designated shipper, the relative's agent in Japan. I make the custom declarations and travel with the body from Kobe to Itami airport."

"The police are releasing the body?" she asked.

"Have already. I mean they must have. The body's at the Consulate."

"I can't imagine it. Think of the forms that have to be filled out in triplicate, all the stuff foreigners have to do in Japan just to live here—the finger printing—the registration booklets. How can they just whisk a body away in a single day?"

"Wells has influence, I suppose. Perhaps they're embarrassed."

"Jesus, they ought to be! It's so absurd. Graham could swim like a champion."

"Maybe not after the gashes."

"I'm sorry I sent you into the middle of this."

"He was something of a friend of mine. At least we talked shop every now and then."

"He was good at that, wasn't he? Jesus, how he liked to talk about his research. How this fit into that, and led to this or that. Jesus! You couldn't shut him up sometimes. And notecards. Piles and piles of 'em. Everywhere. What can I do to help?"

"Come back to the Consulate with me, translate at the shipping office—Pan Am air freight."

"Are they open today?"

"Not usually but to get Guade out of the country apparently all kinds of exceptions are being made."

"Wells at work?"

"Perhaps."

"Say," she suddenly switched tones, "do you mind if I ask you something?"

"No. Go ahead."

"Are you married?" She began looking around again, as if his answer were irrelevant, as if she had asked only to be polite.

"Yes, I suppose so. In a manner of speaking. Yes, married."

"Separated, eh?"

"Yes, as might be surmised."

"Recuperating in Japan?"

"Apparently."

"Most of my *gaijin* friends are doing the same thing. A good place to do it in, if you have money, or, if you don't mind teaching English. Everybody is so helpful, so kind to *gaijin*. And there's plenty to distract you. Just getting around for the first six months takes all your energy, all your will power."

"Yes," Moran agreed, enthused to find an accurate description of how he lived. "I've never been any place where you congratulate yourself on getting through each day so much. I still celebrate, at some level anyway, every successful excursion on JNR lines. How much longer will that go on?"

"Never really stops. You can always switch vehicles once you've got one line solved. When you're not scared of the train system, try some of their roadmaps. Buy a car—dirt cheap before the *shokken*—and spend another year congratulating yourself on that. And then there's the bus system, especially the so called 'Dream Buses.' After that the ferry lines."

"Back to Graham," Moran said.

"It must be the first fatality on that line since the war," she said. "Lousy little seven-hour run from Takamatsu to Kobe in the calmest part of the Inland Sea. I don't see how it happened."

"That's the nature of an accident."

"Too pat. Graham never fell overboard."

Moran studied her for too long a series of seconds, then said "You'd need evidence for a non-accident. It's not like Guade had Japanese enemies, did he? I mean he's got to have been the most obscure *gaijin* in Japan."

"I just don't believe it. Stinks. You can tell when something stinks and this stinks all right. Will you get a divorce?"

The mix of his marital status and Guade's possible murder dizzied Moran. Was one introduced so as to elicit revelations about the other? Perhaps there was some complementarity that she alone held. Moran decided not to answer.

"When is the flight taking him back?" she continued, unperturbed.

"4:00 p.m. But we have to clear customs before 2:00 p.m. I'm to meet Ramden at 11:30 at the Pam Am Air cargo counter."

"We should leave now."

"I suppose. Can you get us there by cab?"

"Better to get a *kyuko* to Sanomiya, then a cab."

"Lead on. We're in the process of a no-fault divorce, agreed incompatibility," Moran said to her back as they rode the first escalator. "Irretrievable breakdown, is the proper term legally."

"Irretrievable breakdown. Has a nice finality to it. I'm sorry."

"So am I."

"You don't want it then?"

"I'm tired of thinking about it."

"Children?" she asked on the second escalator.

"One miscarriage." Moran answered.

She kept her back to him.

"It is irretrievable," Moran continued as they stood on the platform for the Hankyu express. "Nothing angry, bitter, or even nostalgic. Nothing . . . Nothing. Inertial uncoupling. Better to bring this to a stop. Better to stop it before something awful happens. Do you understand? Can you? That's what amazes me. We can't keep working on it. Nothing left in the tank. We just have to stop. We have to draw a line through it. So much to write-off, so much to shovel aside . . . "

"So no real damage, eh? So we can focus on a corpse in Kobe and some grief in Ohio. I wonder how Sanae is taking it. If I can't believe it, what do you suppose she is thinking?"

"She believes it, all right," Moran said, a little startled that Turid knew Guade's wife's name. "She's heard it from enough people. Even her brother Yasunari called to confirm it, although I'm not sure how he knew. She's heard it from enough authority. In a day or so the undertaker will have more proof than anybody could want. You suppose they'll bury him with his hearing aid on?"

"In his expensive shoes," Turid said, looking around again.

Moran decided it was a device of deliberate self-distraction. Scanning the horizon to see if anything might turn up to blot out what was staring you in the face.

The customs official wore grey work pants and shirt, topped by an improbably dark blue military officer's hat. He was not cleanly shaven, as if summoned from a dingy holiday of beer and television in the bowels of Sakai city or some other poor neighborhood in Osaka. He stared at the neatly typed declaration prepared by Ramden's office and said in a thick Osaka accent that Turid had trouble grasping that this was his first body shipped to America. He made three telephone calls. Moran put his *meishi* Japanese side up on the counter hoping that "Visiting Professor" would accelerate the matter. After the fourth call, the official put the sheet down next to Moran's card and said in slow, embarrassed English.

"What's inside?"

"The body, Professor Guade."

"So. So. So, but also, what other?"

"Nothing," Moran answered.

The official looked at Turid, who explained in Japanese that only the body was in the casket. "Where is Ramden?" Turid said to Moran.

"Shoes?" The official asked Moran, pleased apparently with the way he said "shoes."

"Yes, shoes."

"Watch?"

"Maybe . . . yes. Yes."

The official pointed to the sheet, indicating everything should be written down.

This time Moran used the phone. Ramden was still at the Consulate, but promised to do something promptly.

In ten minutes a phone call came for the customs officer, who bowed speaking into the receiver. At the conclusion of the conversation, he promptly stamped the sheet, retained all copies and told Turid the matter was concluded. When they walked out of the cargo area Guade's coffin rested on a fork lift tractor and was moving slowly toward Hangar 119.

3.

They took the bus to Senri Chuo, ate lunch at an imitation Mexican restaurant. Moran ordered enchilada specials, which included a salad and two glasses of rose wine. But Japanese wine was no match for Japanese beer. And they switched to Sapporo Ebisu.

"Who do you suppose Ramden got to call?" Moran said.

Turid cocked her head, "The right person anyway."

"You didn't have to come down here, but I appreciate it."

"I wanted to do something."

"What are your plans now?"

"I suppose I'll take the morning *shinkansen* back to Tokyo."

"Then you can stay over?"

"I thought you'd never ask," she laughed.

"I think you'll like my *tatami*," he said when they entered his apartment.

"So long as the quilts are thick enough."

"They are indeed, and if they're not, I have rubber fold up mattresses for under the *futon*."

"I don't think Graham ever saw those," she said quietly, then she pulled out a plastic chair at the kitchen table and sat down.

"You don't have any?"

"I never thought they deserved *tatami*. Oh I know lots of Japanese use them, but I think they feel guilty adding such Western elements on top of their *tatami*. Some purists think even a *futon* soils their *tatami*."

"And are you 'some Japanese'?"

"When I think about sex, I believe I am. It's natural, almost automatic, like washing your hands before a meal. Nothing exceptional—maybe exceptional now, as a kind of memorial to Graham, don't you think?"

"Memorial sex?"

"Yes, it's grief makes us do it, don't you think?"

"And we're going to do it?"

"I think we owe as much to Graham."

"Were you and Graham lovers?"

"Whenever we could, which was remarkably often—kind of between translations. Once my right leg knocked out his hearing aid."

Moran took a short breath, then a longer one, finally said, "I'll drink to that." He hustled to the narrow short refrigerator and took out two 22 ounce bottles of Sapporo Ebisu. He uncapped both, poured two tall glasses. He sat opposite her at the green sparkling Formica kitchen table. He drank three long gulps.

After a quick supper of delivered sushi and left over soba noodles, and after one more bottle of Ebisu, Moran asked, "How does a little girl from a lonely Norwegian fjord end up in Osaka?"

She takes the *shinkansen* down from Tokyo. Come on," she said, motioned him away from the table in the kitchen and into the *tatami* room. She slid the *shoji* back and began pulling out the bedding. Moran was interested that Japanese sleeping habits precluded uncalculated intimacy. No ruses possible. The low table had to be picked up, legs folded under, and stacked in a corner; the foam rubber mattresses folded in three had to be hauled out, spread on the floor, the heavy *futon* quilt laid over these, then the thinner but still fluffy top quilt put down. Finally two hard bean pillows needed to be tossed on top of the bed.

"Shall we take a bath, an *ofuro*?" she asked.

"Lead on," Moran answered.

There was a hot wait while she filled the deep, small bathtub in its separate compartment within the bathroom. He poured two brandy and sodas. They sipped these until she proposed they undress each other. Moran listened to the steady slow wash of the spigot in the next compartment, while he lifted the black turtleneck over her head. Braless.

"Restraint," she said as he tossed the turtleneck away, pulled her toward him.

"Restraint," she whispered even as he undid his trousers and pushed down his boxer shorts. The remaining removals went awkwardly. There was scarcely room in the main compartment of the bath. He braced against the wash basin as she slowly undid the button of his shirt. Then he moved her over against the adjacent miniscule washing machine to undo her jeans. She was moist but still whispering, "Restraint," when he eased into her, as she leaned back against the washer. "We need to take a bath this way. Can you?"

Moran was breathing hard as she swiveled against him, a mysterious seal shifting slowly in his arms and moving irresistibly toward the bath. "It seems . . . It seems," he struggled for the word. "Extraneous."

"Never. Never. You'll see. Restraint." She opened the door into the bathtub compartment. Steam billowed out of the plastic chamber. They stepped up, she backwards, he forwards, onto the plastic sill. She swiveled a bit to add cold water to the bath. He closed the door.

"One leg each, together," she said, a wondrous, detached sparkle to her eyes. Moran thought, she's practiced in this game. How many came before? Was Graham merely the most recent inductee?

"It won't work. It's too small."

"It will. You'll see."

They lifted legs together, over the high edge of the tub. The water was scalding hot.

"Don't move your leg. Look at me. Pretend your leg has gone down the drain. Imagine that it's out to sea. There. No motion. Nothing disturbed. Let the heat penetrate making its own path. Don't move. Motion makes the heat unbearable. Out alone in the cold grey sea. If you're absolutely motionless the heat diminishes, literally goes elsewhere. Now we move to the other edge so we can bring the outside legs." Searing water rose well above Moran's upper thigh and that pain yanked him out of the cold distant sea.

"Now the other leg, together," she said, taking furious short breaths.

Like a locked pair of herons, Moran decided, they now stood in the *ofuro*. Steam still rising off the settling surface of the water, heat still boiling up through his legs.

"We're still together and we're this far. In our own *caressa*. We're still together and we're this far. Could you imagine it?"

Moran merely panted.

"Now I must kneel and you must sit and we must do it slowly, so that you knees go behind me."

"There isn't room."

"There is. There is. It's the water that is the enemy."

She took hold of the tops of his hip bones, gradually pushed him down as she arched forward attempting a kneeling position while he squatted.

"Your toes all the way to the end of the *ofuro*," she instructed.

The hot water lapped over the edge of the tub, flooded into the floor drain. The heat stung, but she insisted they were going out to sea and that as the water turned darker away from the shore, it would get colder, eventually just calmingly warm.

Amazed, Moran found himself sitting, knees up to the top lip of the water, toes rammed against the end of the tub, and she straddled him and they were still together in the fume of steam and the only now distantly hot sea all around.

"There," she said, satisfied, "such admirable restraint."

"I bet you're a dynamite English instructor," Moran said.

He tried to thrust, tried to find himself at a tip somewhere in the still, piercing heat. But she pushed down harder on him. "Not now. Not now. It will be no good. Just wait. Enjoy the soak. In Japan the best moments come when you stop trying, when you flow with *ki*, when your own movement match the tides unmoving all around."

"You should live in California," Moran said, armpits aflame as they came level with, and then below the bathwater.

"We should always live by the sea."

In a minute, in a year, in three lifetimes, they were standing again, sweating in the steamy chamber, but so boiling hot that even the walk-wobble to the futon was searing. The top quilt was not necessary.

"Now," she said, "we can abandon restraint."

Some time during the night, in the moist fume closeness of the *futon*, Moran asked her if she loved Guade.

"No," she answered, "but I envied him, respected him, and wondered what it would be like to be him—always racing, racing. He had no restraint. And even when he was here, he was always over there."

"And where am I?" Moran asked.

She did not answer, for he had begun to grow again beside her, and he clamped on her lips and probed again, and she responded squirming and meeting him everywhere, so that the bath heat swirling waters left him panting again clinging to the edge of the fantail and furiously watching those churning screws slicing-slashing the sea.

In the morning at Shin Osaka station she stood outside of car 23 watching him as the door slid quietly back. He tried to urge her to get aboard, conscious that the door would close in less than 45 seconds. But she pushed against him, insisted on another moment. She reached into the Funky Babe bag and took out a plastic topped key.

"Listen," she said as the last immaculately suited Japanese businessman disappeared into the blue-white gleam of car 23. "Graham said I should make a judgment and give you this if something happened to him."

"What?" Moran said, suddenly alert.

"It's for a locker downstairs. The real envelope is there. Graham told me on the phone that it was not accident. He gave you the wrong envelope deliberately. But you confused him terribly."

"What?"

"You should pick up the real envelope—that's what he called it—downstairs." She pushed the key into his hands.

"Wait a minute," Moran shouted, but she had timed it perfectly. She crossed the threshold and the car door eased shut. She stared at him through the glass as the sparkling train began its slow glide away. She seemed to mouth, "Don't worry," as he trotted along beside, holding the key up.

Part IV, Ishii's *Hanko*

Even though the platform was as long as a football field Moran knew it was absurd to race beside the train. In six seconds it would be going 70 miles an hour. And the Japanese on the other platforms, forgiving as they were of the eccentricities of *gaijin* might more than collectively frown on the crazy westerner sprinting while holding a lock key on high. Abruptly Moran felt foolish, stopped, thrust the key into his back pocket.

A fool in the morning greylight of Shin Osaka station. A fool, too, in assuming once again that things were what they seemed to be. Guade playing tricks even from the grave. And Turid not apparently the easy, lusty nymph he imagined, but somehow grooved into something beyond Moran's petty facilities of comprehension. And last minute, last second, gambits—to fling him back into paranoia, a state endemic to foreigners in Japan anyway. If you had any sensitivity at all you had to be cognizant of rule-breaking possibilities every moment. And that consciousness could, on bad days, slow you to paralysis. Why venture into the alien world, when merely taking steps would shatter some convention that might be explained to you an hour, a day, a week, or a month later, explained in that sardonic, embarrassed way the

Japanese reserved for discourses on "our customs," or "the spirit of Japanese life."

So Moran stopped, slumped down on a bench, felt the hard key push into his thigh, concentrated on that pain. He would stop running, stop attracting attention and he would think about she had done. With what extraordinary calculation she had done it! Easing him into yet another bath, but this time urging no restraint at all. Had she rehearsed in her mind the little scene of slipped departure—gliding exit, serene behind the impregnable *shinkansen* door? The goddess tosses the hapless suitor at the last minute some nugget for his own destruction: poisoned fruit; the key to the bomb-triggering mechanism. Tosses him her bridesmaid's bouquet, and watches his perplexity, his reservation, his slumping, benched despair. Laughing all the way to Nagoya.

So the "real" envelope was downstairs. The yellow minx at the Shinjuku *turko* had swiped nothing at all. Merely stashed the useless envelope for future confiscation. When he called for delivery, doubtless she checked the contents and took it to be one more evidence of the inept *gaijin's* strangeness. One more validation of his unworthiness. He collected blank pages and socks, carried them about like Government Documents. What else might be expected of him? Better to return the goods and ease him toward the door, then bar it well against his future entrance.

All that remained was to go downstairs, locate the locker and retrieve the "real" envelope. So why not do it? In the first place that would be the expected action and Moran was sad at being scripted by others. In the second place Guade was indisputably dead. Moran had, after all, put his hands into the very wounds. The game therefore was worth rather extravagant stakes to someone. Perhaps Turid's accomplice or accomplices even now were waiting by the locker with whatever twin-screwed devices of destruction they might carry.

Moran got off his bench and from the nearest vending machine purchased a shallow plastic cup of a milk drink sold under the wondrously evocative trade name, "Calpis." Nothing was more startling on Japanese television then the sudden appearance of Donnie and Marie Osmond shouting, "Calpis! Calpis! Calpis!" The drink was cold, sweet, and bracing. Dutifully Moran finished it by standing by the disposal container. In Japan you simply did not walk around eating or drinking. The horrified eyes of the assembled watchers stopped you. Even the stoutest self-actualizing individualist melted under that peer pressure.

When he finished the drink Moran decided to locate the locker, but not retrieve the goods. That, he remembered, was standard procedure in a slew of American crime movies. The bank robber casually strolled by the locker in question. He glanced about and only after four hours of observation did he make the pickup.

The target locker was # 2361, Moran noted, as he turned over the key on the escalator down. True to her declaration the #2,000 banc of lockers was approximately below the platform they had occupied. Everything preplanned then for ease of pickup? The escalator dumped him into a glaring marble floor beneath a solid eight tiered stack of small metal cubicles. Moran began a slow stroll by the lockers, his shoes squeaking on the resonant marble. He assumed he looked unconcerned, thinking apparently only of his destination elsewhere—just one more commuter aimed at a distant platform for another train line. But glancing periodically at the lockers he noted some seemed scuffed to pewter, their green paint chipped off. Passing the 2200s, slowing at the 2300s, but not noticeably doing so, he was sure, he noted that his number was at waist level. He strode on to the end of the banc and knelt beside #2993, pretended to test the key for it. And then he stepped way. He was about hundred feet away from #2361. He eased across the corridor, rested against the tiled wall and looked back. He wished he smoked.

A steady horde of commuters streamed down the corridor. Suit after suit. Attaché case after attaché case. Only an occasional woman in a white skirt and navy blazer jacket—the stewardess look was in this season in Osaka, Moran decided. No loiterers like himself near the 2300 area. No suspicious types anywhere at all, although Moran did wonder what he would designate in Japan as a suspicious type. Perhaps only a *yakuza* with evident tattoos.

So all that remained was to return to the target locker and take what Guade had sent him, however indirectly. But it was too obvious, too predictable. Moran decided against it. He continued along the corridor, took the escalator up and then permitted himself the luxury of a taxi to the university.

In the cab Moran realized she would have had to put the envelope there some time before his appearance at the station yesterday. After 10:00 this morning presumably the locker would open of itself. Anyone might take the contents. He had observed the locker in its last minutes of security. Another stupid miscalculation. Perhaps it would be better to forget everything. What if he never looked at the envelope, never thought again about Guade's death or Atcheson's? Surely the sanest, safest course. On the other hand such a course might close Turid out. And that was to be lamented.

Almost as soon as he got to his office on the dingy third floor of the filthy building housing the Faculty of Literature, Moran commissioned the lone English speaker in the Administration Office to return to Shin Osaka station and bring the envelope back to him. Moran warned the fellow that the locker might be open, in which case he should have to check the Lost and Found. He decided against warning about explosions.

"Hai, wakarimashita!" the fellow replied.

At noon he brought a sealed manila envelope to Moran in the faculty Common Room. Moran put the envelop on the seat beside him, finished his tea and his "English Conversation" with a younger linguistic scholar who wanted to know if the expression, "Tell it to the dragon puppet," was a popular saying in America, especially in New York. After some reflection Moran decided to say "Yes," to that question and any that might follow.

Moran shared an office with an older, silent scholar who was, apparently, Japan's foremost authority on English dictionaries created in Japan. Unfailingly polite and distant, the scholar occupied a desk opposite Moran's with an obstacle, back-to-back bookcase between them. Usually the fellow slept with his head on his desk, or Moran heard him swiveling his chair to reach the small gas space heater, kept perfectly equidistant from their work areas.

Moran took his seat. Slid out three envelopes from the large manila one. The largest interior envelope was brown and neatly labelled, "To: Professor G. Guade c/o The Fulbright Commission in Tokyo with a return a return address: The Air Force Inspection and Safety Center, Norton AFB, CA 92409/ The cover letter from Colonel Petelchuk to Guade explained that a review of the reports indicated 56 pages were releasable and were enclosed at a duplicating expense of $12.75. Three categories of information the review had decided were not releasable: first, "the investigating board's opinions conclusions, findings (including determination of causes and recommendations) are not releasable. This information is exempt from disclosure under 5 U.S.C. 552(b)(5).

It may be withheld under the statue and regulations because the release of such information would have a stifling effect on the free and frank expression of ideas, opinions, and recommendations between Air Force officials." The second category included testimony of witnesses given under immunity, and the third involved the medical records of victims. Only light check marks were in the margin next to these. The final paragraph was circled:

"The decision to withhold release of the portions of this report, described above, may be appealed in writing to the Secretary of the Air Force within 45 days from the date of this letter. Include in your appeal any reason for reconsideration you wish to present and attach the enclosed copy of this letter. Address your letter as follows: Secretary of the Air Force through HQ AFISC/DAD-T, Norton Air Force Base, California 92409."

Below this Guade had written in ink, "Appeal sent 11 days after receipt. Copy attached." Moran skimmed the one-page appeal. Guade did mention the similarity of language to Watergate rhetoric (hardly the most cogent argument it seemed to Moran) and closed by lamenting the "Air Force's continuation of the confusion, misperception and conspiratorial speculation concerning the 'China hands' by refusing to release the board's findings."

The remaining pages appeared to be the typescript of various rescue unit conversations , the original orders cut in Tokyo assigning personnel to Flight 4576B, and then, peculiarly, a set of five photographs showing lifeboats in a grey shiny sea—really nothing more than puffs of light on the grey surface, apparently photos taken by rescue planes. Parts of the rescue transcripts were underlined and Guade had written small paragraphs near a section detailing a conversation between the USSCG cutter Hermes and a rescue unit referred to as "Hayride Fox."

Moran opened the second envelope which was labelled, "Captain Sigmond and Nosaka" on the outside. There was a single 5 by 8 inch notecard inside, as well as a typescript on onion skin paper of a conversation between Guade and Nosaka, apparently a carbon copy of the original. The carbon was smudged a bit and it was easier, Moran decided, to deal with Guade's meticulous script on the 5 by 8 card. There were three entries on the card:

1. Captain Sigmond does not appear on the HQ orders for flight personnel issued August 12, 1947 signed by Willoughby acting on behalf of MacArthur.

2. Flight Roster issued on August 16, 1947 shows Captain Sigmond as third flight officer added to military personnel aboard.

3. Who is Captain Sigmond? Answer—one of the 4 lost and never recovered from the pacific?

Moran put these back in the envelope and opened the third one, marked on the outside: "Scenarios." Inside there were three folded pages torn from a yellow, legal size tablet. The first page had been marked into three segments horizontally. Moran shifted the page around on his desk top. Segment one was labelled, "Accident," and had listed below that title a number of items: "The times account, the SD issue, the summary and findings of the AFB investigation. Plane runs out of gas and ditches in rough seas. Sinks. 8 accounted for directly, 1 seen to sink. 4 lost unaccounted for. But the AFB's assessment is not available. Check fuel consumption charts, docs, pp. 17-20."

The second segment was marked "Suicide," and under it Guade had listed Moran's name with a question mark after it.

"The Communist-exposed rationale. Cf: notes for conversation with Wells and evidence given military by Nosaka. Is this valid evidence Note cards 34-147?" There were no notecards in the envelope. "Review of Atcheson's file."

The third segment was marked "Murder," and below appeared Captain Sigmond's name followed by "OSS? G-2?" and then, "Nosaka's statement given to Turid and Guade. Flight accident report? Refusal to release same?"

At the bottom of the page Guade had listed questions and then apparently speculated on some answers himself. There were two paragraphs in minute, careful print:

"What is the relation among these three versions? Are these the only three? How fit the three together? Atcheson fell victim to accidental death, was himself slain by history moving randomly. The 3rd engine failed, then the second, then the ditching was poorly done (inevitably so in 4 foot seas) and the sharks pursued no random savagery. The seas closed on Atcheson and the sharks took him out of history. But version 2 has its advocates, Wells, the leading voice. The secret Communist about to be exposed. Atcheson finds himself in the perfect situation for a final acting out of despair. After all, charges had already been levelled. It remained only for the questionable dispatches to be published or leaked. Wells indicates that was in the offing via *Amerasia,* or some other magazines. And Atcheson knew he was coming back not to discuss MacArthur's actions or a possible peace treaty with Japan, but to be relieved. So there was the angry, inviting sea. A solution to all sorts of problems, and, as a bonus, a double indemnity clause of Government life insurance. The Harry Dexter White route? Final penance for the elations of the late 30's? Final expiation for too close collaboration during the Grand Alliance of WWII. Atcheson's hysteric anti-Communism in Japan only a cover then?

"Or the rationale of murder. There are no accidents in history, says Nosaka from his hospital room, from his creaking, bed-cranked exit from this world. Atcheson was onto some game, the carefully covered game, and therefor had to be eliminated. What game? But Nosaka lies as it suits him, or, as he shouts, as it suits history. Then it was important to discredit the China hands, and now the military. Nosaka smiles as he explains to Turid how Atcheson discovered what he did. Then what does Moran truly know and how are Wells and Moran linked?"

Moran considered underlining the words, "What does Moran truly know . . . " Evidently, nothing. Who, after all, was Nosaka? What was Wells but some removed patrician that one might orally interview to fill out the details of a thesis already generated from the documents. What dealings could Moran have had with Wells? That Guade imagined commerce between them immensely amused Moran. To be included in the history-making imagination of Guade was a signal of significance. What linked Moran with Wells? Apparently the off-hand statement that Atcheson may have been a Communist, a sentiment Wells apparently accepted and orchestrated into a perfect self-destruction for Atcheson. But why? Guade must have been trying to find out on the way to Shikoku. Would the accident to Guade explain the accident to Atcheson?

2.

That night Moran called Turid fully expecting no answer, yet worried that if connection actually occurred he could not really trust anything she said. There was something wildly enticing by that prospect, more arresting than any memory of a shared steaming bath.

"Are we actually talking?" Moran opened. "Can I accept anything you say? And if accepting, what comes of it?"

"I thought I had timed it just about perfectly." She answered, with a whispered chuckle at the end of the thought.

"Who's Nosaka?" Moran said.

"He's dead. Graham interviewed him two years ago—we did, since I did the translation. He was the senior eminence of the Japanese Communist Party—jailed in Kyushu for most of the war. The militarists thought he was a traitor working for Stalin. And he was, I suppose, or at least Graham thought so. Graham never believed anything he said. He had some funny ideas about Atcheson. MacArthur used Nosaka to establish new worker unions. Graham thought it was hilarious how MacArthur loved unions and at the same time loved the Republican Party in the U.S. You could tell me why that was hilarious. That was Graham's term, 'hilarious.'"

"I'm not sure hilarious is the right world. Maybe it applies to us."

"Why?"

"Here we are dancing around corpse, passing locker keys in a way that precludes explanation—trying to figure out what's going on and who's using who. Was Graham using me?"

"He never said so, and I only did what he wanted. Everything."

"Yeah, that's pretty clear . . . are you saying 'everything' meaning 'everything'?"

"I do what I want when I want."

Moran listened to that declaration while watching the strangely out of place, quaintly small bamboo forest behind his building sway in a sudden breeze as if to fan her statement with a beguiling stroking pleasure. Moran eased back down into the hot, hot bath. "You sound like my soon-to-be ex-wife." And when Turid didn't respond, Moran said, "Did Graham have directives in mind for me? Things he wanted me to do, things to research."

"He said once, he'd hoped you'd take on talking to someone named Petelchuk at Norton Air Force Base in California, someone he'd been writing."

"I saw some of that correspondence in the envelope. He felt Petelchuk had Atcheson's 123 file. I don't why he would have it. I could follow up. Care to come along?"

"To California?"

"Yes. Air Force bases there are legendary."

"I don't think so."

"The bases, or travel with me?"

"We do better with the shinkansen door closing quickly."

Although his sliding glass doors were closed Moran knew the bamboo forest in full tilt made a delicious sighing noise—a shimmying dismissal of his disappointment. Wind through the thick upper leaves bent the bamboo stalks to its will. He'd read somewhere, or perhaps some thrilled undergraduate told him, that Japanese often tied prisoners to pegs in the earth over growing bamboo trees and watched as the stalks punched through the writhing bodies. Still he remembered the white hot bath water cresting his crimson kneecaps. Turid's deception was somehow entirely freeing. And Moran was amazed to hear himself say: "I don't care whatever game you're playing. Just keep playing it and let me watch, let me be the victim of your frolic, if it is frolic. I'm enjoying the run—you know when you're running over pointed rocks near the shore and you can't stop because if you stopped you'd lose balance and cream yourself on the granite, so you keep leaping ahead from one rock peak to the next, to the next, to the next until finally, finally, there's a blessed flat spot where you can stop running. It's like that with you. I like the way your hand feels—it's so soft, so keep gaming me. When you're doing it, I feel really, really alert—about to burst. Do you understand? We're in an ever-hotter bath, aren't we?"

"You only have to flip the handle and the heating stops."

"Let's not flip the handle."

"Petelchuk said he has the 123 file, and Graham could come and look at it any time."

"So come with me."

"I can't. I'd lose my students, my *gaijin* learning Japanese, my Japanese learning English, even one learning Norwegian. I can't set them aside."

Moran thought but didn't say, "When you're on the rocky points and running, everything is set aside. . . everything." Guade always knew what to set aside, didn't he? Until someone came out of nowhere, and set him aside.

And when Moran was on the flight to Los Angeles, there was an Indian woman in the seat to his right. She wore a burnished brown sari, and evidently her two young sons occupied the rest of the row. There was small glowing amber jewel in her forehead. For an instant Moran wanted to brush it aside. He imagined brushing it aside would render her naked and together they were in an ever heating bath. Instead the four of them slept quietly until an overly dry, unevenly warm quiche was served in its peach-colored plastic dish.

3.

To the guard at the gate Moran pointed to the notice Guade had received and said, "Professor Graham Guade to see Colonel Petelchuk, appointment at 10:40 a.m." Moran hoped and imagined his crisp military style certitude would carry the day of deceit at least to the office for a meeting. I perhaps should have worn a hearing aid, Moran thought, and beefed up a bit while at the same time flashing hidden energy resources through restless gesturing. Having been waved on, Moran began to fantasize that Guade doubtless drove with a certain thrust. Guade trusted his intuitions and his data collection. Moran wondered about both. With, he believed, military precision Moran threaded the rental car past buildings until Barracks 155 turned up, flanked by cabbage palms and dust plumes periodically obscuring the striking mountains beyond. There were four empty parking places.

Moran kept up his charade, telling the receptionist at the front desk and the one outside Petelchuk's office, that Professor Guade had arrived for his appointment. For a moment Moran imagined going through with the deception to the very end—mentally sampling a certain arrogance from past achievements, fantasizing himself as a trenchant scholar tirelessly ferreting out the truths of the past, and flipping conceptual frames as needed to realign data that threatened the arches of true knowledge. If he could sample Guade's mistress why not his celebrity? His acumen? His very prospects in the dying field? But Petelchuk quickly re-established order.

"I see you've come back from the dead. How amazing!" Petelchuk said, coming out from behind his large, walnut desk and striding directly at Moran.

"You knew?" Moran actually back stepped, scrambling for a cover story.

"He was well known—his death made the papers on this coast, probably the other one too. Who the hell are you?"

Taking one more step back and then two to the side, Moran said, "A colleague, fellow researcher. I actually put Graham onto the problem of Atcheson's death. I got him interested in the issue. He begged me to continue the leads he developed, if anything should happen to him. Before he left for Shikoku he asked me to follow up with his translator in Tokyo. I felt it was the least I could do. She's very skilled." Moran smiled and Petelchuk stopped advancing. "I do apologize for passing myself off as Guade, but he had the appointment and I don't think as David Moran, historian, I would have gotten through the gate. But everyone assumed I was Graham. It was a deception but undertaken at Graham's direct wish. If you want to throw me out, I fully understand, but Graham really wanted to look at Atcheson's 123 file. He felt everything would fall into place if he had access to it. That's why I'm here."

"Now, fancy that. You're the third fellow here in the last two weeks asking to see the 123 file. Can you tell me why?"

"It shouldn't take long. 123s are usually just birthday greetings, notes from kids, wedding invitations. Two other fellows? Historians?"

"I didn't ask them. State Department said, let them look. I let them. One of them said most of the stuff was in Japanese. They both photographed everything. So I began to think there's something interesting there. Is there? Maybe you can tell me. I'm supposed to send them to the National Archives, but I'm thinking something about this 123 file is especially interesting. And now you come along pretending to be someone else and now I'm thinking. What's interesting here maybe can be monetized in some way. Can it? Should it? Or maybe somebody's career is on the line—some scandal that could be difficult for advancement. And I'm wondering why should these blessings fall to me, and what do I need to do to capitalize on this largess. A good word, largess. I doubt I knew it before you all came into my life. All these thoughts keep occurring to me."

"Monetize?"

"A figure of speech. If I wanted to shake people down I'd be more discreet setting it up, wouldn't I? I mean I wouldn't be such an asshole as to pretend I was someone else. I wouldn't under false, and incidentally arrestable basis, come into a military facility of the United States Air Force and pass myself off as somebody else. Only a very dumb shithead would try something like that."

"Or a dumbshit who might have access to higher levels of your chain of command," Moran said levelly.

Petelchuk stared for five seconds, watching Moran's eyes carefully. Apparently, Moran surmised, he was calculating a response that had opened a small window on Moran's probability. What did the captain see through that window?

"Okay, let's play hardball. I'll call patrol and get you arrested and you can summon your blessed higher levels of my chain of command. Let's just try that, what do you say?"

"I only want to open the 123 file long enough to take my pictures. I'm number 3 on your gift list and your ass is covered since State told you to do it—offer it to anyone who came calling. I'll bet you didn't query State again when number 2 turned up all anxious for his time at the trough. So why bother asking about number 3? Just give him his twenty minutes, and then send everything to National Archives, according to orders. And be done with it. Done with it. Or would you rather I share with you whatever I eventually find, so we could, as you mentioned, 'monetize it.'? But I should say at the outset—I don't read, don't speak Japanese. That will be taken care of in Tokyo with Turid."

"What do I care?"

"So you'll let me have a look? A foto or two?"

Petelchuk went to his door, opened it and said something to staff on the other side. He was handed a thick rhubarb-color, expanding folder. "The others photographed on that table," he pointed to an empty white collapsible table at the far end of the large office. "Under the LED light. Apparently perfect light. And watching them I thought what's really going on here? Whose ass is on the line? Guade seemed really fired up about something. His faxes laid out all sorts of arguments that I should release the final report on the crash and recommendations, as if I had that authority. I don't. I'm just here for the duration. For the duration. That's a military phrase for getting out, don't you know?"

Moran quickly sorted through and set aside about twenty various birthday cards, then three clippings from the Scranton Gazette chronicling Atcheson's career at key appointment moments. There were Christmas cards, Thanksgiving cards, Easter cards across several years all penned by obviously very young children, expressing how much they missed him. Sudden sadness flooded up in Moran, regret he and Natalie had never even tried to have children. But quick tears receded as the large package of handwritten Japanese turned up amid the dumped file shards. Moran arranged the pages on the table top and began photographing. "Anyone say what the Japanese pages discuss?"

"Anyone?"

"I mean numbers 1 or 2 specifically."

"Number 2 said he wrote the passages."

Moran stopped, said, "What did that mean?"

"It meant he wrote them. That's clear enough."

"Was he Japanese?"

"Hell no. Irish, red-haired, and pretty fucked up."

"But able to write Japanese . . . "

"Yeah, that was . . . was unexpected, eh? At least I thought so. He didn't explain why. Just snapped away. Didn't make much sense. He wrote it. He had to know what it said. So I assumed he was photographing it for someone else, but every now and then he'd blurt out, 'Oh, Daddy!' and then again, 'Oh, Daddy!' That's when I went back to my desk and unlocked the bottom drawer where I keep the Glock."

"You felt he was unstable?"

"I don't think so, but I wanted protection within easy reach. You know this is described as a 'career ending' assignment—a little resting place so you max the pension and slide into a golfing oblivion. I look forward to it, but now all of sudden the SD becomes part of my end game. And for what, or better yet, for why? What's going on that suddenly my salad days end up smelling like kimchi?"

"I'm sorry your last days are so mephitic," Moran said, half laughing since he imagined Petelchuk had never heard of the word.

"Take your fucking pictures and get the hell out." Petelchuk said slowly, sighfully. He went back to his desk and opened the top drawer on his right.

For a moment Moran thought the Glock might appear, but he realized he'd erred with his vocab display, and now there was little to do but obey the Captain.

"If you're interested I can tell you a little something about the Japanese stuff," Moran said as he started to leave Petelchuk's office.

Petelchuk spun his chair away from Moran and addressing the mountains in his giant window said loudly, "Why not?"

"I recognized the *hanko* on each document, even though I don't read Japanese. It's Ishii's *hanko*—"

"Are you talking about bread crumbs?"

"*Hanko* is a personal stamp—you use it to sign personal documents or to indicate something belongs to you. The Japanese don't use signatures, they use *hankos*. Ishii was the head honcho of a huge biological warfare lab in Manchuria during World War II. The documents have something to do with Ishii and his operation—maybe personal copies. Medical stuff, maybe data from his experiments. I can't tell. Turid probably could, but even she would have trouble with this technical crap."

Petelchuk turned back toward his office door. "You know something? I really, really don't give a shit."

"Fair enough," Moran agreed, "but I have one more question. How far and in what direction is Rancho Santa Fe?"

"South, about an hour, maybe two." Petelchuk answered. "So number 2 interests you most, or is it just because he's nearby?"

"The latter."

"Better bring a Glock."

"That bad, eh?"

Petelchuk spun back to his mountain view. "Good luck to you, Professor Guade, or whatever. God speed your mephitic ass."

Part V, Hesseltine's Interim

On the drive south Moran wondered whether Petelchuk really didn't know anything, or was just playing the end-of-career-carefree drone bee cruising inevitably toward final freedom. Petelchuk's mix of dismissal and deep interest seemed more than a pose—rather a pique of enthusiasm always throttled by the irrepressible bridle of imminent retirement. There was no sense scuffing up the fairways and greens of the next steps—wasn't that always so? Still, why at the last wicket did so many players appear? Each one pledging to "send him away" with their mallets swung so freely and unguardedly? Perhaps he's worried that one of end-times mallets carried extra weight—a sock of lead? So there he was under foot at the wicket's edge, just to be whacked elsewhere, deep into the rough.

But, Moran thought, Petelchuk was not the worrier type. He dance stepped through the last challenges confident satisfaction was either directly in front of him, or so thoroughly distant as to exert no charm at all. His was an engagement that Moran envied—fully present yet entirely absent, the supreme observer of a game in which he had no stakes at all. And doubtless the players were off beat and partially enveloping so that they could be manipulated and tested without consequences. Was that an ideal life, Moran wondered?

But there was too much distraction—natural wonders as hills materialized and scrub shrubs grew thicker as Moran passed beyond Escondito and into the rocky lush landscape of Rancho Santa Fe. At an immaculate Gulf station Moran asked about the address, 231 Calvin Drive, and the attendant, a young Mexican fellow in a crisp, starched white short sleeved shirt immediately said, "The Oxley place."

"Really?"

"Oh yes! The best view ever. Once you're on 31 take the second fork to the left and follow it up the hill all the way to the top. That road ends at the Oxley place. But they aren't there—they went to Italy."

"Really?"

"Oh yes! Maybe a month ago. Maybe they got a house sitter. My sister does that for the hill people sometimes."

"I guess I'll find out. Tell me about the 'hill people.'"

"Rich. Some even grow tea."

"Really?"

"You use 'really' a lot."

Moran studied the attendant for a moment—was there hostility in his observation? Would an apology defuse the situation? Or maybe he was just saying his English mastery was at least equivalent to Moran's. So brushing aside the speculation, Moran asked, "And the Oxley's are rich then and tea growers?"

"Definitely rich. You'll see the house. It's rich. Willy Oxley is rich. Peg Oxley is rich."

"And in Italy . . . "

"Right. In Italy."

"Rich in Italy," Moran continued. "Something devoutly to be wished."

"Oh yes!" the fellow agreed.

On the other hand when Moran got to the Oxley place he wondered why anyone would want to leave it. The view across the other hills and valleys was puffed occasionally with cloud banks that moved so fast the revealed greens were intermittent. The edge of the open garage's roof dangled baskets of bougainvillea that seemed to march around the structure. A jeep and two Mercedes filled the spaces. Moran threaded his way among them to the open walkway to a very solid looking cherry door. But before knocking Moran scanned the vista once more, wondering if the patch work green spreading beneath and away from the garage represented tea plants or some other dark shrub. The squares were so neat, so cultivated Moran imagined there must be a battalion of Mexican farmers at the Oxleys' command. Then fog puffs settled in partially blocking the view, then lifting, then crossing the cabbage palms closer to the house then moving swiftly across Moran himself—a moist moment of anti-sunshine. How could Italy compete, Moran wondered? He gently rapped the knocker, surprised by the muted tone he generated. He snapped it harder. There was no response. A long drive for nothing, Moran thought. He left the walkway and went around the back of the house discovering that it extended further than he imagined. At length he came to a side flagment patio, with more hanging bougainvillea plants. On a third flaming orange lawn chair set entirely flat there was a fellow on his back with a San Diego Times spread over his face.

Moran coughed with enough force to command attention, but the newspaper didn't move. So Moran said, loudly, "Nice place you have here."

The newspaper slid down a bit and the fellow's eyes came into view. He was squinting and seemed in some kind of pain. "Do you think I own it?"

"I know you don't. I'm Graham Guade, a friend of the Oxleys. I drove down from Escondito to check on their place. They asked me to do that." Moran suddenly delighted in how easy it was. Yes, he could be Guade, the energetic, the focused, the relentless ferreter of truth. "Should I call the police?"

"I doubt they'll come since Willy told them I'd be staying here, drinking their wine—a really nice Riesling by the way—and walking barefoot through their very thick camel's hair carpet. You should try it. It's orgasmic."

"I take it you're an old friend of, of Willy?"

"I'd guess you don't understand how Presbyterian missioners live in this world. So let me tell you. They move from one posh house to another, never letting the dust settle on their sandals—they carry no bags, aware always that their lot is only ashes. Just ashes above the tea plantations. Ever been to the hill communities of India? Cool and comfortable—no malaria. Like here. And wherever you go, there we are—Presbyterian missioners—summoning the guilty rich back to blessed self-abnegation. Blessed recognition of their ungainly gain. Want some wine? It's really pungent, with lush complexity." He fumbled around beneath the lawn chair and sent two empty bottles toward Moran's feet. "Ah sorry, seems I drank up the outside stuff. There's more in the refrigerator. Could you get a bottle?"

"It's a bit early for me."

"Good God, a teetotaler . . . "

"Not exactly. And not exactly a Presbyterian swiller either, I guess."

"Oh God, you're not going to add to my guilt and sin, are you? A guilty house-sitter cannot be effective."

"You seem to be doing all right."

"Can't complain. Let's have some wine and tell each other appropriate lies. It's going to be a terrific day here in the hills. In fact every day is terrific. Even northern Italy can't match 'em. I have no idea why Willy and Peg wandered off. We can count our blessings until they return. Do I really have to get up to get the next bottle?"

"It's okay I'll do that honor," Moran said, opening a slider and entering the kitchen.

After he came back and glasses were poured, Moran said, "I suppose you know I'm not Guade. Captain Petelchuk certainly knew."

"Frankly I didn't care one way or the other. Still don't. I got what I was after—Ishii's notes, or at least copies of them. Photographs of them."

"Why did you want them?"

"They're proof. Absolute proof."

"Proof of what?" Moran asked.

"I wonder if you're as dumb as you seem. You don't know who I am, do you?"

"Archer Hesseltine, the second fellow to look at Petelchuk's file—Atcheson's 123 file."

"That's right. That's good. We can build off that, can we?"

"I don't know. Can we?"

"Apparently not much. So let's not try. Let's just drink a bit, talk a bit. Maybe sleep a bit. Maybe sleep a lot. I do have one question, and I'd like a straight on answer—no fooling, no foolin' around. None of that, right?"

"Yes."

"Good. We can agree you weren't sent here to kill me."

Moran was startled by the way Hesseltine stared at him.

"I think we can agree on that," Moran said.

"You're a little slow answering that. Should I be worried? I mean were you thinking it over? Debating it? Weighing it somehow?"

"I'm sure. I've never killed anyone. Is someone trying to kill you?"

"Okay. Let's have a smoke." From under the thin flat pillow at the top of lawn chair, Hesseltine took out a fat cigarette. "It's Thai, very good shit, incidentally." He took a full toke and passed it to Moran. "I've got a couple of peyote pods too. We can make the next twenty hours go by sweetly."

"To going sweetly," Moran said sucking smoke in. "I haven't done this in fifteen years."

"Your loss. I do this every noon, every evening. I'm whole for breakfast. For Jesus."

"That's nice."

"Maybe," Hesseltine said, "my Daddy was whole for Jesus, twenty-four seven. Twenty-four seven."

"Probably breakfast is enough," Moran said, watching carefully as a cumulus small cloud wafted up from the valley of tea trees. He remembered the wobbling stilts of initial draws fifteen years ago—the magic relaxation of sinews, tendons slow melt, the way cartilage seemed to snuggle down against bone joints as if to lick away any abrasion. Sometimes Moran imagined he got the same quick relief from three quick gulps of a gin and tonic made at a five star hotel some place in Asia, but that always had a certain heaviness to the thrust. This was like releasing a kite, and staring up to trace its arc but not seeing anything at all, and realizing wanting to see the path was absurd. And then the wafting cloud cottoned over him a near perfect sanctification of cool evanescent mist. Then sharp sunlight and the need for another hit.

"This is some place, Rancho Santa Fe," Moran said with sly silly affection.

"Wait till you feel the camel's hair carpet between your toes."

"Not now," Moran said. "Not now. I want to stay here. Outside."

"That's interesting," Archer said, "Willy Oxley said the outside was always beckoning but you had to be very careful—always wear heavy shoes, chukkas or maybe even boots—Willy always wore leather boots. Because . . . because," losing the thread a bit. "Because, it's necessary, absolutely necessary to kick over anything you plan on picking up. Necessary because scorpions are always under things. But I've never seen even one. Let's eat. I'll make some deviled eggs. I live on deviled eggs."

"Not yet," Moran said, "give me another hit." He took three quick tokes, lungs to bursting, then slow release through clenched teeth in soft hissing sighs. "Really good stuff," Moran said finally. "Really good."

"It'll do," Hesseltine answered.

"Who are you and why are we in this idyllic place?" Moran asked, relaxing flat onto his lawn chair. He thought he saw a hawk circling overhead, but it could have been something in his expanding eye.

"Because Unit 731 fucked us up. Fucked up Guade. Fucked up Atcheson. Fucked me up royally. But I don't think it touched you." Archer answered. "I make my deviled eggs with curry powder, lots of curry powder—almost gritty you can feel the powder smearing over your teeth. You think it will dissolve, but it won't; it'll click over your fuckin' teeth and settle into the back of your throat and its fumes will light the yokes up so that they glow going down."

"I don't want deviled eggs."

"Oh you say that now. But you don't know what you want until hunger starts. You'll beg me for my deviled eggs, as soon as your body sends you a signal—eat, for God's sake eat. Eat everything. Suck everything in. Lick the grit on your teeth. You'll beg me for my deviled eggs. You don't have any idea what Ishii's *hanko* means, do you?"

"Bread crumbs." Moran said. "They also click on your teeth, isn't that so?"

2.

It seemed to Moran at least two hours passed as they assembled material for deviled eggs. Running water for the cracking of eggshells—gentle waters swarming over the flecked off tiny pieces, and the endlessly infuriating way certain large shell pieces clung so fiercely to the delicate sheer white inner skin lining the egg. Moran tried to tell Hesseltine that the experience was a metaphor for something, perhaps life itself, but Archer was too busy dropping three peyote pods into a small pot of boiling water. When that cooled he offered a glass to Moran.

"Takes about twenty minutes and you'll throw up before it kicks in."

"It kicks in . . . " Moran said slowly stirring some curry powder and mayonnaise in a brown cup. He added eggs yolks. "I don't usually like to puke."

"Who does? But if you want to get beyond the Urals you have to take the train."

Moran finished the drink which tasted acrid and sour, like sauerkraut or Moran imagined a smoothie made from sun-soaked, abandoned avocado rinds. He rocked back and forth stroking the powder into the smashed yolks and mayonnaise. The curry fume carried up his nose to the back of his throat where it summoned Indian restaurants remembered blissfully.

"I don't suppose Willy keeps Kingfisher ale in oversize bottles here, does he?"

"We could look, but let's not. It would be pushing our luck."

"Yet you seem to be a fellow at ease in pushing our luck."

"I'll think about that. Are you feeling the beginnings of nausea?"

"No," Moran said slowly, interested in the sound of the word. "No . . . no. Who was Ishii?"

"I told you. He was the commander, the commander of the unit. Unit 731. He created it. He ran it. He kept it going. He did the experiments on the *maruta*, the logs. He killed the logs. Thousands of them. He killed them by the hundreds, by the thousands, by the hundreds of thousands . . . maybe. Especially the children . . . the children, and the pregnant mothers. He killed them. He experimented on them. He sliced them up. He froze them fast or slowly. The children. He left them outside in minus 30 degree weather. He injected them with glanders, or cholera, or polio, or anthrax. We could look for Kingfisher in the wash room. Willy has a big freezer there."

"Sounds like a plan. Let's definitely do it. And you're right about the nausea."

"Feel it coming eh? Always the anticipation, that's the worst. Ishii said the kids had terrible anxieties when he sunk them in water barrels outside. He wanted to see how long it would take to freeze them to death, and if it would be faster if you wounded them. Such knowledge would protect the troops, don't you see that? That makes it all right, makes it important, makes it medal worthy, doesn't it Daddy? They were just *maruta*, weren't they, Daddy? Just logs . . . toss them on the fire, Daddy. Toss them on the fire."

"The kids were called *maruta*?"

"Not the kids. They weren't the logs. Anyone knew that. Anyone. I think there's an opener hanging by the freezer, on the left side. On a rawhide lanyard. Willy is way into rawhide."

"Did you know Ishii?"

"How could I? I was in the fucking army. I wasn't in Manchuria. But I knew him. I translated every fucking note he took, every lab book, every speculation. And here it is—22 ounces of India Pale Ale, the king of Kingfishers. Give me the opener. Detach it from its tethering rawhide and give it to me. I need it. I have a use for it. Ishii liked twins. Need more twins, he penned in the margins. Need more twins. 22 ounce twins. But here there's only one. Willy has failed us. Willy disappoints me. Does it every time. Every time. We need to advise him about his purchasing. He needs to buy two or four of everything. Isn't that so?" He took a long swallow from the bottle, then handed it to Moran, who waved it off.

For Moran the floor began to undulate, and then, with rocket quickness, vomit gathered itself thrusting upward squirting out through his clenched teeth—a further golden green spewing that fully opened the teeth and puddled near the stainless steel freezer. Archer, laughing and taking another swig of the beer, slipped on the wet floor and piled into the freezer door, dropped the bottle, grabbed at the long steel handle and lowered himself to the floor which had shot out from under his sopping shoes. Moran joined him, sitting in the slop. But it was as if he were on a skateboard noisily coursing up and down over the undulating flagments. "Oh," Moran said, "can you slow the floor down?"

"No. Of course, not. No. Ride with it. You have to. You really have to. Breathe and ride, ride and breathe. If you yell that only tells them it hurts, which is exactly what they want to know. How much it hurts, how deep to cut, how far to slice. If you add salt to the water will you freeze faster? Will you? If they put an ice pick into your chest can you indicate at what depth the pain becomes acute? Is there a word in Japanese for 'acute'? And what is the 'diarrhea norm'? Are we living in it?"

"Yes, "Moran answered, "we're living in it. Living in it."

But Hesseltine began crying, a weird muffled sobbing that had him gathering some of the puke up in his hands and slowly examining it, squeezing it as if it were some kind of clay that irritatingly wouldn't congeal properly. Still squeezing his fingers together, still sobbing, Hesseltine at length said. "We forgot about the eggs. They're alone in the kitchen. Alone and frightened, I know it. I feel it. Alone and terrified. Can you hear them screaming?"

"Fuck you," Moran said, "eggs are inert. They don't scream, and besides I can't get up."

"But they're alone and frightened. I can see them in the notes. I'd have to take time off. I couldn't just keep translating and translating—poor children freezing to death. Operations without anesthesia, just to see if they could be done. At what age would the shock be too much? Research for troops in the field. How to spread disease germs effectively for maximal impact. And you won't even attend the eggs. The lonely frightened eggs." Suddenly Hesseltine righted himself, stood tapping puke off his trouser legs, and said, "Fuck the eggs. They're dead already. They just don't know it. Fuck them and their screaming."

"I'll attend them," Moran said, retching once again. "I'll stop their screaming."

"Do you see into the stainless? Do you? I can. The steel dissolves into a great maroon color, a soft pudding. Look I can stroke it. Watch my fingers rile it softly. Look at it. It's matchless . . . matchless . . . "Hesseltine smiled widely, too widely. "Without fire, unneeded ignition . . . matchless!"

"Come out of the steel and join me making the eggs," Moran said, lurching in comic flailing toward the kitchen.

"Fuck the eggs. They're dead already. I've written them up. I know the temperature at which they died. I know the minute their breathing stopped, their involuntary convulsion commenced. I've gotten down their blood pressure's quick descent and when precisely their vocal cords wet with salt water froze blocking all speech. Exited all screaming. I recorded when their eyeballs turned up and iced over. You think you mashed them with your stupid fork and your smelly powder but they were dead already. And because they were young and unformed they only looked quizzical choking to death, or maybe just startled at their own bloating."

"I'm growing taller," Moran said, "I'm fucking growing like bamboo. I am bamboo. I'm shooting up. Look! I'm against the ceiling. I can see you down there. I could stomp on you with my heavy, heavy, foot."

"No you can't. Take the fucking shoe off and feel the camel's hair—two maybe three inches thick on Willy Oxley's carpet. Camel's hair delight. You can chew it, if you like. Does that interest you? Ever think of chewing the carpet? Ever dream of eating Willy Oxley's carpet? I think about it all the time."

Moran in fact knew he'd grown. He scraped along the vaulted plastered ceiling 40 feet above the thick, orange-colored carpet. "I can barely see you Arch." Moran called out. "You look piddling."

"Piddling," Archer answered. "Piddling work. Every lab page translated, transcribed. Recreated. Every operation described. Every death itemized, every medical moment noted.... and noted. . . and noted and transcribed. Medical Japanese is a nightmare for translators, did you know that? Even Daddy knew that."

"I could crush you with my giant foot," Moran said delighting in his perspective amid the ceiling's bridgework. "I'm not only up here, I'm growing down to support my enormous and growing body—my elongating body. Look at my leg going down to support me, to keep me up here."

"You're in phase three," Hesseltine said. "And it's boring me."

"You'd rather do your translations—itemizing what? More medical experiments?"

"Cholera in the countryside, dropped from the air. Anthrax delivered by pigeons. Ishii tried them all. Them all." Archer said slowly, sinking into the orange carpet, submerging, Moran thought, into the camel's hair.

"I'm thinking it's difficult to breathe up here."

"You're beside me and you're breathing fine."

"I'm not. I can't breathe easily. I have to plan to breathe. I need to will each breath. It's not good. Not good at all."

"It's fine. Discard the anxiety. You know what you're doing. You're apart from it. What you're writing down doesn't make you part of it."

"What are you talking about? I'm not breathing. You've got to help me breathe."

"I can't help you. It's just a phase. They'll see what happens when they fill your lungs with the fog and don't worry it will pass. You'll come out all right, or you won't. It's not my concern."

"Are they filling my lungs with gas?"

"Of course they are, my child. They have to. They have to see how it incapacitates you. Troops need the information. Maybe just enough. And you'll come through it, or maybe you won't. And I'll have to write it down in English, even though English is not my native language. I'm a freak translator. Ishii's apprentice."

"You worked for Ishii?"

"No. Of course not. I worked for Atcheson. I translated Ishii's notes. I'll get you a bag."

"A bag to die in?"

"No. Not at all. I bag to breathe in. You're over breathing. You're beside me over breathing in the camel's hair. You're hyper-ventilating. And I have the cure. It's standard. It will save you. Do you want it?"

"I want something."

"Of course you do. Something to make it easier. Here, take the bag. Open it. Make a collar with it. Put it over your mouth and breathe into it. It will save you. It will make things better but you might die anyway. And I can't help you. I'm 800 miles away, and in another time. I'd make it better if I could. But I couldn't. Atcheson couldn't. God he wanted to. God did he want to. Are you breathing into the bag?"

"No. I'm fifty feet above you."

"Well, come back down. Float down slowly. Slowly. I'll try to help you. I will, especially if I can't fathom the terms, can't find the words—the awful words. Even my Dad didn't know the words, never encountered the words. If I had elastic arms I'd reach 800 miles and take you up, cradle you, and the pain would subside, but I can't. I'm trapped in another time, just reading and writing the words. It's horrible. Just reading and writing the words, translating the words. The intermediary."

"I'm not coming down. I'm not. I'm dying—that's what I'm doing."

"Well, of course! Get on with it. Find the words. Finish the assignment and leave. Leave."

"I can't breathe. How can I leave when I can't breathe?"

"Put the bag back over your mouth and breathe into it. Do it now! And do it proudly and quietly. Slow. Slow. The slow steady accumulation of details, details after details. That will turn the trick. That will make everything right again. How he believed that."

"Ishii?"

"No. Of course not. Not Ishii. Atcheson. He wanted every detail. Every piece of evidence. Translation of course. But beyond that photographs, and there were. There were photographs—mouths stuck in agony, wide open screaming, eyes glistening with pain, blood from ears, and severed arms, torn open bellies, gangrenous feet, blackened limbs and eyes popped and frozen, marbles on a bench. And children retching everywhere, dizzy with fever or frozen solid. I translated them all, every page Ishii *hanko-ed*. And Atcheson shouting he had the proof he needed to undo the whole effort."

"What effort? Breathing into this bag? Is that what you mean?"

"Yes. Of course. It's the effort that Daddy listened to and denied and denied and denied. But he couldn't. I could show him photographs and Ishii's documents. And he couldn't say anything. Saying nothing just standing and looking at me and then shuffling away, kicking Shikoku dust so that it lifted upwards around his sandals and ankles. Lost in the camel's hair carpet, like us. Good God it's thick isn't it?"

But Moran, having filled the bag, suddenly recognized where he was and how much he was disoriented, near vomiting again and so sorry for swallowing whatever it was he had swallowed. What was it? Mescaline extract? Psilocybin? Apache mushrooms? Guade's relentless ferreting? Hesseltine's whining father confrontation. None of such things. Clearly there was craziness here. Nutso chaos galore, and the important thing was to crawl away into some quiet exit chamber, some safe harbor for the next nausea wave. The thick carpet made crawling labored and worrisome, as if you might never get off the mangrove into safer deeper water. Moran knew Hesseltine was totally unmoored, pinballing among Ishii's documentation, Atcheson's imperatives, Guade's pointed questions, Daddy's apparent expectations. Moran only knew the place was sun-struck and utterly loony. Time to exit. Time to flee. Get up and run. Cranking upwards, balloon legs extending down into the orange hair growing taller by the second. Heave forward, and then topple, topple gloriously into the soft golden earth.

By the next afternoon the nausea had given way to a rather pleasant, near constant undulation—a kind of sea shore sense of being washed up and back on a liquid stainless steel beach. It seemed natural and inevitable that part of the motion would entail talking again to Captain Petelchuk. But of course he could not be easily reached. In fact it took, Moran noted, four explanations, and five insistences to thread the way through the bureaucracy's telephonic labyrinth.

"Stop complaining about the difficulties and give it to me on the horn what you want," Petelchuk said as Moran imagined the sea was made of mercury and could curl waves that might not actually lop over.

"The first fellow's name. I failed to write it down. The one who came first to look at the 123, who was he?"

"Jesus," Petelchuk said. "He was young, a researcher, maybe grad student—a punk. I don't carry names around in my head. Why should I?" He broke off and Moran heard him yelling at the office staff outside door. "Okay, okay. It was Thomas Cole. Tom Cole. Nice kid. Earnest. Are we done?"

"Did he say who sent him? Who he worked for or reported to?"

"I don't remember. Somebody at the State Department or maybe his grad school."

"Think harder." Moran said almost laughing. There was something magical about the phone line: he could be a bully with impunity. That was terrific. What could be better than ordering Petelchuk around? Maybe just lying in the sun and contemplating the mercury curl wave that never collapsed on you . . .

"Be serious," Petelchuk cautioned. "I think he said some Emeritus professor asked him to look at the file, something like that."

Moran pounced. "Livingston Wells, perhaps?"

"Maybe. Sounds about right. How should I know?"

"Do you want to know what the Japanese notes were?"

"Not particularly. I sent the file back to archives."

"Lab notes of experiments in human atrocities—biowarfare shit. Genocide experiments. Live vivisections on *marutas,* Chinese prisoners, foreign captives, probably some Americans. Nauseating stuff. Really nauseating stuff." Moran could get hand and toe holds on the towering mercury wave. He could pick and pull his way to the very top, yank himself over the curl and suddenly see, a thousand miles away, hazy mountains. Petelchuk amid the peaks was beckoning to him.

"I think I saw some of that stuff at Fort Dietrich."

"Really?" Moran felt himself suddenly focus. "Was it in Japanese or English?"

"What do you think?"

"I really don't know. I really want to know. I'm serious."

"Yeah. Swell. Signing off." Petelchuk said.

"You can't sign off on this shit," Moran said slowly, but the line had clicked dead.

From the kitchen Hesseltine shouted, "We didn't eat the eggs. They're right here, looking terrific. Made with care and focus and wonderful turmeric fumes. The lonely, perfect eggs."

Archer held one out to him. "California mayo never spoils," he explained.

Moran swallowed the egg, felt rising nausea and sprinted through the mud room to the outside. He knelt in the grass and wait for the vomit to rise, but something in the cool, mucid air tamed things down. Even the heavy undulation subsided. The lawn took on a beguiling soupy texture and Moran imagined he could comb it, if he had a large enough, widely spaced enough comb. And imagining how such a large and widely spaced comb could be generated from a multi-toothed plastic spewing machine, Moran collapsed over on his side, then his back on the lawn and watched a very distant cloud bob out of sight. Had the comb merely cleared slowly through the sky, collecting the hapless mini-cloud like a beetle swept out of the sullen maiden's carefully combed hair?

3.

Around 7:00 p.m. he called Turid in Tokyo, waking her. Since her opening "Moshi, moshi," seemed so groggy, Moran immediately apologized, muttering and listening to the sound of "gomen, gomen, go . . . men," with a wondrous fascination. He decided a large crowd could in fact chant slowly, "Go Men! Go, Men!"

In eventual exasperation Turid asked, "What drugs have you been taking?"

"Whatever Archer doles out, and they're prolific, and, and . . . nauseating."

"You woke me up . . ."

"Gomen, Gomen! I wanted to let you know I'm coming back with documents. Ishii stamped documents, but I can't read them. I need your help."

"Who is Archer?"

"Another file snatcher. Atcheson's translator. Like you— my translator."

"Not yours. Graham's. And he paid, paid well for everything I did."

Moran turned that phrase over in his mind, slipping his leg into a wonderfully hot bath. "A business relationship?" Moran said slowly.

"It's a little early to lead you to maturity . . ."

"Okay, okay. I admit I'm a little still up there, a little deranged, but I'm coming down fast. I feel it. Talking to you is really helping. Helping is the key. I need your helping."

"I understand you're a bit wasted. Are you?"

"A bit."

"So you need to listen. Listen carefully. Thoughtfully. Hearing slowly and well everything I'm saying. That way I can be really helpful. Can I be really helpful?"

"Yes, you certainly can."

"And how can I be helpful?"

"If I listen carefully to you. Isn't that it?

"Yes, that's it. So listen carefully."

"I'm all ears." Moran said, suddenly infatuated with the vision of himself as a collection of ears arranged on the lawn in a large question mark. Were the ears tanned? Should they be? He wondered if Willy Oxley's ears were beet red from so much exposure to the sun. Moran muttered, "Willy's ears were burnt."

"Dismiss Willy and listen to what I'm saying. I have information for you. Perhaps key information. And I have another, much better, much more competent translator for you."

"Someone to sort Ishii's lab books for me?"

"Yes, precisely, and someone very anxious to see you, very anxious to help you. And not too far away."

"But far away, anyway." Moran said fixing now on the thrust of the conversation.

"Not too far away. Fluent in Japanese, written, medical Japanese. And very anxious to talk with you. Someone who has called here twice begging to see you."

Moran drew back instinctively, "No one wants to see me," he said slowly, twisting the sound in his mind. "No one."

"Once again feeling sorry for yourself," Turid chided. "The isolated child. I'm tired of it. It goes nowhere. But somehow makes you feel invulnerable, doesn't it?"

"Does not."

"Are you still listening?"

"Yes."

"Good. Take this down."

"I'm on the lawn and without instruments," Moran chuckled. "Flat on my back and without a pen or paper or anything for notation. But I have a first rate memory, I think. Maybe people have mentioned that to me. Sentiments like, 'You'd be nothing without your memory.' Stuff like that."

"Maybe you should call me back tomorrow."

"No. No. No. Just tell me the information, and I'll remember to write it down when I go back inside, if I ever do that."

"Okay, 1217 Fourth Street, Columbus, Ohio. Got that? Sanae wants to see you. Got that? 1217 Fourth Street, in Ohio, Columbus, Ohio."

Part V, Hesseltine's Interim

"Columbus, Ohio. That's far away," Moran said, imagining a map across the continent.

"She really wants to see you."

"Sanae does?"

"Yes, she does."

"And who is Sanae?"

"Sanae Guade."

"He never mentioned her. She's Japanese?"

"Duh . . ."

"That's not true. He mentioned her once, but I thought she was someone on staff at Kyoto."

"No, David, it's Sanae Guade, Graham's wife—a great translator, perfect for documents of long-ago atrocities. What could be more perfect? And she wants to see you. Really wants to see only you, David. Can you imagine it? Sanae thinks she can explain what happened to Graham. She has notes of what he was working on. She has memories of conversations. She's convinced it was no accident."

"No accident," Moran repeated slowly, savoring the sounds. "No, spelled with a 'k'?" he asked.

"Maybe we should talk later, after whatever has worn off."

"That's the gem of it. It never wears off. It changes the layers of synapses in your brain so you can see things no one else thinks to see. Thinks to see. Think about that. Thinking about thinking to see."

"Call me when you get to Columbus. You owe that much to Graham. Think about that." And Turid hung up.

The large phone receiver suddenly seemed overwhelmingly heavy and Moran flopped in on the thick lawn. What could he possibly owe Graham? The allegiance of the indentured grad student bound to finish the master's final work? Hardly. Nobody but Guade did Guade's work—his saturation in the sources was stuff of convention gossip, as was his chary selection of only the fewest acolytes. The first requisite was the ability to challenge the master, dispute his findings, offer alternative explanations, endless rebuttals. The required ritual hazing made only the strongest yapping dogs acceptable to force the master further up on the achievement pole—Guade needed the constant nipping at his feet on the ascent. His seminar was the last bastion of loyal opposition. That role bored Moran, but in the data collection Moran began to see the possibility of a second book on the hapless China Hands—a biography of Atcheson, to compliment Moran's sturdy, tedious exposition of Clarence Gauss. And lengthy interviews with Guade's widow, a first look at Guade notes on Atcheson, a first encounter with Guade's conceptualization of how the game unfolded, his first speculations on Atcheson's motivations and actions would surely be more than a leg up on potential challengers, and a firm entrée into better publishing venues. Yes, a new biography of Atcheson might rescue Moran's unmoored life, adrift in Japan—marriage sacked, children ruled out, nothing but the tepid *gaijin's* near endless sipping of hot sake in winter, cold in summer, one long eventually unconsumable strand of soba, threading up the hapless *gaijin's* total detachment from care. Comb the sea, comb the steel lawn, and those mercury static waves, comb on, Moran. Surely a whiff of Columbus would re-emblazon purpose, direction, stability and who might predict what would happen after a Sanae-sample? Sanae represented rescue and rededication. Moran howled toward embracing it.

Part VI, Sanae's Grief

There were surprises in Columbus: Guade's home; Sanae's sad diffidence layering her apparently frail beauty; and a child—a three year old boy bobbing in Guade's dingy house like a cork in dark, unattended water and now seemingly more adrift than even Moran after Guade's removal.

The house on 4ᵗʰ Street was nothing appropriate to a historian with Guade's reputation and sales—a very modest and dilapidated two family, almost but not quite a shame on the street; stacked porches in need of paint and restoration, the railings on the upper level riddled with gaps and rain eroded edges. The grey-green paint only half completed so that the prior brown stain dominated the north side of the building. Meticulous research nowhere evident. Moran sympathized with Guade's conference-hopping, and what he imagined were constant late stays at the university. Who would want to come back to such a place? Perhaps only a well wrecked Hesseltine, or Petelchuk, just for three weekends per year—surely not the meticulous, energetic Guade.

"It was always next year's project," Sanae said without a trace of Asian accent. "But Graham always found a better research project, and I'm always busy with Denny." She pointed to the boy in overlarge shorts not really disguising his diaper.

He rocked to left and right left to right and stared at Moran, as if trying to make him become his father, or that seemed the case to Moran. The boy's revisioning stare disconcerted Moran.

"No staring, Denny. What did daddy always say about that? No staring. It's rude," Sanae said, and then whispered, "Perhaps autism, we're not sure. They're not sure. No one's sure." The boy had to have heard.

"How old is he? Graham never mentioned him," Moran answered with less quietness.

"Because of his differentness," Sanae said.

Moran thought—of course in Japan the word for "different" was also the word for "wrong". It was always better in Asia to hide your errors, your sins, your accidents of fate. Make the house blend in with the neighborhood, maintain it just enough not to call attention to it, and, above all, keep the embarrassing child hidden. Moran had seen cot-lined warehouses in Taiwan for disabled children, safely walled off from view. In Hong Kong there were attics for the dysfunctional, in Mong Kok garages loaded with cast-off relatives. In Japan maybe things were better in distant rural retreats, and in Columbus, quiet ignorance and an attic sealed room—was that the case?

"Thanks so much for coming. I was so hoping you would. Graham constantly talked about you as the only colleague he trusted. No one else knew what Graham was working on. He always said you were ahead of him, guiding him—" She turned from watching the boy and her eyes took on a look that Moran thought recessive or dimly lit somehow as she talked of Graham. Her eggplant smooth skin seemed to lose its resilience and partially bleach from its natural color.

Moran said, "No one was ever ahead of Graham. I surely didn't guide him. I barely understood what he'd found, or even what he was looking at." Moran thought about adding: he hardly was forthcoming, in fact more than a little bit paranoid, spreading deceit wherever anyone might have begun to understand what he was doing. But he imagined Sanae wouldn't have, couldn't have, heard such sentiments. Moran stared (rudely) at Denny wondering what might be happening in the boy's brain. But Denny, apparently tirelessly, rocked in place toward the left, then the right.

"Please. Have some tea. You must be tired from all the driving." She plugged in a metal kettle smudged with fingerprints and water streaks, shoving it back a bit as if to hide it. "Is bancha all right? It's all I have now."

"Bancha is perfect."

Denny moved in front of the narrow, white refrigerator. He cocked his head to the left, but his eyes fixed on Moran.

Disturbed by the boy's stare Moran said, "I found the drive restful, after a pretty weird encounter with a fellow named Hesseltine in California. You know I had planned to go back to Japan, but then Turid called saying you really needed to see me. That was a God-send. I wanted to get away from Hesseltine."

"Oh, I'm so sorry to put you out, to delay your return. Graham was going to ask you to see what he had saved here, but . . . but . . . " she trailed off.

"I was so happy to have an excuse to leave Archer Hesseltine—did I say he was weird. Did I say that already?"

"Yes," Sanae answered softly. "Graham thought he was pretty strange—like a lot of long term *gaijin* in Japan."

"Graham had met him?"

"I don't think they met, but Graham spent hours on the phone with him."

"How did that happen?" Moran said, suddenly alert.

"I'm not sure."

"I mean how did Graham find out about him? I only stumbled on him at an Air Force base in California. I can't imagine he moved in Graham's historical circles. He actually seemed loony to me, or maybe just perpetually stoned."

"Graham said he sounded addicted."

"Well, yeah! In a very big way. But I don't get it how Graham knew about him."

"I'm not sure, but I think someone at the State Department mentioned him to Graham."

"At State?"

"I think so."

"You don't have a name?"

"Maybe an Under Secretary, . . . maybe."

"Liv Wells?"

"Look around. I don't think we do live well. Do you? Graham said he was a *henna gaijin*."

"I suppose I'm becoming one too, although only a couple of years in old Nippon."

"Graham didn't think that. He trusted you, didn't he?"

Moran thought a bit about that, had formulated a guarded answer, part hostile for Guade's game playing, part envious for his intensity of inquiry; his absolute focus, to the point of almost comic dismissal or anyone on the lesser frequencies. And in the soft grey light of Columbus late afternoon, here was evidence of the abandoned shards of ambition. Moran liked the sentiment. At least I didn't leave behind such wreckage, he thought and then remembered what he had left behind or pushed away or somehow not ever grasped. More likely never had. Sudden self-pity wilted before a sudden lurch into an imagined encounter between Guade and Hesseltine—what a bizarre show that would have been. Searching questions and double fey answers. Catastrophic phantasms sputtering before demanded footnote documentation. Martinet focus amid deteriorating flower power. A waltz of dysfunctional behemoths, embracing in the wind-driven sunlight of Rancho Santa Fe. But of course it never happened, did it? Coming up for air, Moran said pointing to rocking Denny, "Does he talk?"

"Oh not yet. But he understands our talking, our thinking."

"I doubt he understands what I'm thinking. I'm too tired to know myself."

"I think he knows that. But I have to give you what Graham promised. I had to deliver it only to you. That's a reason why I wanted you to come. He was very precise—I had to hand it to you directly. That's how much he trusted you."

"And distrusted everyone else. That's really odd, you know. I constantly had the feeling Graham was testing me to find out if he could trust me. He gave me ambiguous directions, had me pickup documents that turned out to be new socks. Yes, socks stuffed in a manila envelope. I always thought he didn't really trust me with anything. I had the constant sense that if I could do A he might trust me to do B, which would be required before I could be given C. And now you're saying he wanted me to get personally some materials he was using? Is that what you're saying?"

"Graham was using you? Is that how it felt?" Sanae said, turning and watching the small parking lot of an auto body shop beyond the kitchen window. "Denny and I know about that feeling. We know all about that feeling." There was a surge of conviction in her voice that startled Moran, as if all vestiges of initial meeting, initial fox trot of dialogue had suddenly been set aside. "He gave you tasks to see if he could stop erasing you—treating you like something he needed to employ, is that how you felt?"

"I'm a little tired, and when I'm tired I tend to feel exactly as anyone describes me, if they're forceful enough . . . "
Did she sense that umbrage, as if she had stirred memories of Natalie—or more likely his own fatigue at laboring under another's characterization?

"I'm so sorry. Of course, who wouldn't be tired after such driving?"

Even an insensitive asshole like me, Moran thought.

Sanae continued, "Please rest, but I want us to talk again tomorrow. Come for breakfast. Graham was not what you think . . . not what I thought. Not what Denny thinks. Right now, I'll give you— I'll put into your hands, just as he commanded—the folder, the file he'd assembled. I will faithfully carry out his wishes, and after that tomorrow we can talk about Graham. You have to promise me you'll come back."

"Oh absolutely! I didn't drive all this way not to get the full message. I'll come back, and we can talk as long as you want, as many days as you want. I'll be like the man who came to breakfast."

"I don't understand."

"There was a play, maybe a T.V. program called 'The Man Who Came to Dinner' about an old fellow who was invited to dinner and ended up staying for years, and running the family's life, making all their decisions, helping them all grow up."

"Like Graham," Sanae said, then turned and went out of the kitchen. Denny watched her exit. Then he turned, stared again at Moran, and stopped rocking.

"I don't think you know what I'm thinking," Moran said softly to the boy, and in a mocking playful but perhaps sinister way began rocking himself.

Sanae came back with a bulging brown folder, looped with an elastic tie. "Well, here it is. And with it I fulfill Graham's last request."

She said the phrase with a certain relish Moran immediately sensed came from some anger. He assumed she resented a secretarial role.

"I'll take it and read it tonight, or early tomorrow morning. And I'll come back and we can talk about it."

"Graham wouldn't have done that," Sanae said. "He wouldn't have seen the use of it. How could a discussion with me affect anything he was planning?"

"Yeah, well . . . yes. See you for breakfast, perhaps a later breakfast . . . "

"We'll be here just as Graham left us. Just as he wanted us. Just as he refused to see us." She spoke crisply but it seemed her skin tone faded and the luminous brown of her eyes simply lost any hint of energy.

2.

The wonderfully named, Ohio Motel, was only two miles from the 4th Street address. Room 114 like all the other rooms had a musty brown shag wall-to-wall carpeting, a 17 inch T.V. massive cube sitting on a polished black desk opposite the twin beds. Moran promptly flopped on the bed nearest the sliding glass windows and fell asleep. He dreamed he was in a canoe with Sanae and Denny and, strangely, a yipping brown poodle dog. As the pond turned deeper and more resonantly brown, suddenly Sanae took her paddle and swatted the dog forcefully, knocking him off his stance at the bow and into the brackish water. Then Sanae regained her balance and clubbed the animal twice on the head so that blood flowed and the poodle turned belly up and floated away from the canoe. Moran woke up sweating. He turned on the right side of the twin goose neck lamp between the beds and then opened the folder Sanae had given him.

The sheet at the top of the first rubber-banded packet was labelled: "male child, age 11 (*maruta*)—freezing monitor, right arm dismembered, at 12 minute mark, death by minute 22., approximately 3 minutes longer than twin brother out of the tank, but restrained outside, in -33 degree weather and not dismembered. Immersion in salted water may retard freezing, despite open wound? trans. by A.H. September 23rd, 1945." There was a drawing of two boys, one chained to metal post in the ground and beside him another boy submerged in what seemed to be a wooden rain barrel, with a concrete barracks-like building in the background. It seemed the boy had been strapped into the barrel. He couldn't move. A prominent circle at the right bottom of the drawing simply listed a minus 33 degrees. The drawing showed the boy in the barrel with his right arm lopped off at the elbow.

The second sheet listed: "February 12, 1941—female, age 26 (*maruta*), 5th day after direct exposure to anthrax powder. Difficulty breathing, sensitivity to probe. Vomiting every 30 minutes. Death at 11:20 p.m. 5th day. Trans. By A.H. October 3, 1945." There was no drawing, but at the bottom of the sheet there were numbers which to Moran seemed like blood pressure figures, and pulse. At least such numbers fit his assumptions. Below them was a hand written note: "These are just summaries. I need the actual translation of everything on the document—everything, numbers, test results, etc. If necessary (and probably it will be necessary) add Sumi to the task. I need details!" signed "ga."

The 3rd sheet followed along the same structure: "March 23, 1943. Male, age 46. (*maruta*). Glanders direct injection, 8 days prior. Writhing on bed, vomiting, and considerable bowel discharge, mostly bloody. Intrav. Pen for 4 days. 175/100/96. Death at 9:17 a.m. amid bloody discharge. Trans. By A.H. October 7, 1945." At the bottom of this sheet there was a hand written, faint pencil note: "Arch, get the doctor's names for each, if possible. ga."

The 4th sheet began, "witnessed by Dr. Tanaka, removal of liver without anesthesia (field conditions)—straps pulled tight, strained. Copious blood. Patient writhing and howling. Death after 14 minutes. Blood loss or trauma? Male, 51 years old (*maruta*). Dr. T pointed out that duplicate of field conditions was faulty. Trans. A.H. October 20, 1945."

The 5th sheet noted: "K attended, girl 9 years old. Acute cholera. Continuous bowel discharge. 12 day. Intravenous solutions, and death in the seventh hour of the 13th day. K stayed with the body for over an hour. Trans. By A.H. No clue to K's name."

The 6th sheet was labelled, "Vivisection of pregnant woman, age 29 (*maruta*) . . . " and Moran stopped reading, turned off the light. Passing traffic illumination flickered around the drawn shades and was swallowed up in the dank carpet, the black desktop. Moran listened to his own quick breathing, and for an instant thought he heard, and deeply welcomed, the sharp swat of a flailing canoe paddle. There was an imagined shock of collision and he slumped back in the flimsy bed, tossing the thin pillows on to the shag sea.

In the morning the brown carpet felt mucid under his bare feet, vaguely oily—something not washed off by a shower in orange tiled upright coffin with its frosted swinging door. On his way to Sanae's Moran checked out alternative motels. But he doubted change of place would alter how he felt.

"When you understand fully that those you love cannot actually see you, hear you, cannot understand anything you actually feel, the carpeting means nothing." Sanae said. "I know the Ohio Motel. I stayed there a full week without Denny or Graham before he went back to Japan this last time. Graham brought me Denny on his way to the airport. I knew the relief Graham felt by delivering Denny to me. The amazing freedom I'd been feeling for that whole week, despite the guilt of leaving them both." Sanae deftly stirred a cast iron skillet of beaten eggs as she talked, moving the black silicone spatula in and around the steadily drying out yellow mass. "I could tell he was back again into his work, the steady piles of data, the endless collection—assembling the tidbits. I knew that look on his face that utterly erased anything calling him away from that rush to collection. Stupid assembling. Worthless accumulations. And meanwhile here we were, Denny and me, totally erased, little stupid props on the stage of his efforts toward accumulating, assembling, whatever."

Moran could see the gathering upset and wondered if grief drove it. Or was that too hopeful a spin on her words? She seemed to have advanced beyond anger to simple dismissal, a not yet celebrated freedom because, after all, she had to recognize despair underlay her feelings. She plopped a large clump of eggs on Moran's Currier & Ives plate. She motioned to Denny to come sit at the porcelain white metal table, but the boy didn't move from in front of the refrigerator.

So long as I'm around, he merely rocks back and forth, Moran thought.

The boy's motion entered Moran's perception, sluicing back and forth, his own view of Guade's home life and Sanae's motivations. Her smile at him signaled he knew, from watching Japanese women, dark anger some place, but he couldn't find it without a lot more careful listening to her. And that seemed profoundly tiring, an exhaustion he knew at bottom was the laziness Natalie had always said was uniquely his.

"Are you saying you actually left him and Denny?"

"I did. Just before he went to Japan. He knew what he was coming back to—nothing. Just like the nothing he had reduced us to. Do you want ketchup? Americans like ketchup on everything."

Moran forced a chuckle. "That was a cheap shot."

"This is a cheap life." She answered. "My brother said Graham was crazy for collecting. Never hearing, never assessing, just collecting. It's what he lived for. He never saw us other than our saddling his obsession. Yasunari saw right through him. Told me to kill him or leave. How can you live with someone who deeply believes you just get in the way? And Denny only made that clearer. We did both get in the way. We still get in the way."

"Not in Graham's way any longer," Moran said trying to sort out the depth of Sanae's hurt or anger or grief or maybe just her delight in saying in a foreign language what she perhaps couldn't even imagine in Japanese.

"I can still feel his disappointment in having to think about us. He projected it onto everything we did or thought. Isn't that so, Denny?" She put the skillet back on the stove and went to the boy, embraced him. "We don't have to care about this man, Denny. We don't have to care. We can be shut of him."

Moran noticed they both began to tear up. She took up his rocking motion. They fused in Moran's blurred image, and for no reason he could imagine, Moran suddenly said, "I dreamed last night we were all in a canoe and you swatted me with the paddle and tried to kill me."

"Yasunari would have done that!" Sanae laughed, releasing Denny and suddenly turning buoyant. "Yasunari saved me, saved us!"

"Saved you?"

"By showing me it didn't have to end as I imagined. It was within my power to change it all."

"It has changed," Moran said.

"He's still not listening," Sanae sighed. "But Denny doesn't care, do you Denny? When he's not here we're free, aren't we, and he's not here. Not ever here. Not ever again." Sanae began crying and Denny stopped rocking to watch her.

"I've only made things worse," Moran said, eating his eggs.

"I'm so sorry," Sanae said. "I'm so sorry."

Abruptly Moran got up from the table and put his arms around Sanae and the boy who had clutched at her waist. It was an involuntary gesture of empathy and Moran felt himself backing away from it, a novel impulse that unbalanced him momentarily. "Look," he heard himself saying, "grief is hard and surprising—regret carries everything before it. Don't worry. It will clear. You'll find something, some way. Some way. Some way." He repeated it gently as if to believe it himself, but the boy released and began rocking again. Gradually Moran's hold on Sanae became embarrassing and to cover he also released and said, "I'll finish Graham's work about Atcheson, about everything." What was everything, Moran wondered?

"Oh, I don't care. Denny doesn't care. Who could care?" Sanae answered turning toward the sink and letting the water run. She watched the water swilling into the drain—a metaphor Moran decided was more arch than real. Still staring at the descending stream, Sanae said, "Graham thought Mr. Atcheson was going to expose something when he got back to Washington and what happened to him wasn't an accident. He was killed."

Moran wondered if Guade had rehearsed her. He imagined Graham holding her arms and saying slowly, "Here's how you tell him, as an aside, as relief from some other revelation, some other hurt, so that it will seem realer than it might be if you had just said it straight out." But of course she said it straight out.

"Did Graham say why? Or better yet, how? It was a plane crash and most survived. Atcheson didn't. Pretty hard to get a murder out of that."

"I don't care. He said he wrote his theory in his notes on the Hesseltine translations. Something about someone joining the flight in Kwajalein and not surviving along with Atcheson. I don't care. But Graham thought you would. That's what he charged me with. That's my obligation to him. The last act of love, and his dismissal, his erasure," she said bitterly, taking hold of Denny again. The boy burrowed into her hip and clamped his arms around her waist, and gradually a low moan emanated from him, a moan that swelled brilliantly into a whining scream, a torrential house-shuddering howl such as Moran imagined one of the two boys in the first sheet's drawing might have issued as bloody ice congealed around them. They all froze together—the severed arm the first to solidify but, anon, Moran, Sanae, and Denny joining the tableau with Hesseltine moistly chuckling as he drew the scene.

Soon enough Sanae calmed Denny down, by picking him up and forcing his mouth into her neck, stifling the scream. She looked around involuntarily as if checking to see no neighbors had come running. And having made sure no one was judging her, she slumped down onto the metal chair at the table.

THE GAME IN THE PAST

When it seemed her ministrations had sent the boy into sleepiness, awkwardly arranged against her lap, half on the chair, she said, "That the saddest part. He really misses his father who could only erase him . . . erase and erase him . . . erase us. He really misses and loved him. I can't understand it."

Seated opposite her Moran brought his palms slowly down his face and simply nodded. He sighed an offered lamely, "Nobody understands children, especially since we didn't have any."

"Did you want to have children?"

"I didn't and eventually Natalie didn't either. It was one of the few things we agreed on." Moran said and then added, "But it was a loss. Natalie was superb at itemizing those."

"I can't be Denny's father," Sanae said apparently oblivious to Moran's revelations. "Even when Graham wasn't fully here, he was at least someone for Denny who loved him beyond all reason. Beyond all understanding. Love smothers erasure, do you believe it?"

"I'm not sure. Smother sounds ominous."

"I will smother you, Denny." She took hold of the boy again and hugged him, still crying. "I never saw my parents kiss," she said kissing the top of Denny's head. "And now he won't get even his father's quick kisses. He won't ever get them. He's all I have of Graham. More than I want." She pulled Denny tighter and then said to Moran, "Oh, finish your eggs."

"They're cold and undercooked," Moran said smiling, pushing them away.

She half laughed and said, "Graham never liked the way I did them either." She brushed away some tears. "Yasunari wants me to come home."

Moran quickly added, in the sudden wonderful mode of familiar lecturing, "My experience of Japanese women who have been in America more than four months is that they never want to go back home. And you've been here years. So I suspect you don't want to go home."

"I don't want to be watched again, constantly observed again. And Denny? What kind of life could he have in Japan? Half *gaijin* freak who might never speak, and without a father to protect him."

"My sense is that children need no protection in Japan. They're safe everywhere. Incredibly safe."

"I meant from bullying, since he's different—not uniform, not Japanese."

"So stay here."

"Here and utterly alone. Alone," she seemed to savor the pronunciation.

"And if you're alone in Japan, you're dead. All *gaijin* in Japan are dead, but only a third of them know that." Moran was transported to that magical professorial declamatory range beyond the silk blue sky, above all self-conscious clouds. "That's why I don't stay on. The money's better. The life's better. It's safer. American bleat can hardly be heard. But here I am. In Ohio."

"Here we are," Sanae said, guiding Denny back to his spot before the refrigerator. "Here we are and without Graham organizing our lives. Well, perhaps not organizing my life any more. I'm not so sure about yours," she added.

Moran watched the boy who once again began rocking. "True enough. I'm hooked enough to get a biography of Atcheson out of Graham's rummaging around. Hooked enough. Maybe the suggestion of dark conspiracies would increase trade sales. Maybe I could get free of university presses. Maybe that would be nice. Graham certainly must have enjoyed it."

"It's all he cared about." Sanae said. "Only Denny got in his way. So I became more and more Denny. More and more Denny. More Denny. Maybe you should go somewhere else where they cook the eggs properly."

"Maybe we both should listen to Yasunari," Moran answered, stung that his banter could be so boomeranged.

"Yasunari wants me to cover his crime, to live in the shadow of his action on my behalf, and let Japan devour every last bit of me and Denny."

"What action are you talking about?"

"His rescue of me from the clutches of Ohio, out of the rough *gaijin* hands. Graham's grinding erasure. He wants me buried, Denny buried as consequent burden, recognized and celebrated burden. It will give focus, purpose, self-celebration to his life. But it won't happen, will it?"

"I doubt it will," Moran answered, actually wondering what might ensue, and still confused by what she was saying. "Maybe I should just focus on Atcheson and what Graham wrote about him. Maybe I should retreat into history and give up on life—at least my life understanding your life." Moran smiled and tried a half laugh.

"Denny and I have to do our shopping anyway. So go back to the documents. Maybe you'll be like Graham, on fire with new revelations, new speculations. Maybe you'll be happy sifting for nuggets. Will you?"

"Hesseltine's translations of Ishii's stamped sheets are pretty nauseating, pretty sickening. I doubt there's a nugget anywhere in the collection. Only one atrocity after another—deranging stuff. Really deranging stuff. I think it overwhelmed Hesseltine, deranged him."

"Graham said he had finally made sense of it—something about Atcheson's motivations. He didn't want my . . . my involvement, my feelings. He surely didn't want that."

With sudden jauntiness Moran said, "And now you don't have to fret over that issue. Our beloved President Calvin Coolidge once said, 'If you see ten troubles coming down the road toward you, you can be confident at least nine will run off into the ditch before they get to you.' Words to live by. Graham's safely in the ditch." But at those words Denny began a wheezing howl again.

3.

At 2:00 a.m. from the Ohio Motel, Moran called Turid . "I really needed to hear your sane voice, your well-adjusted, un-grieving voice."

"I was about to call you, too. I needed to. Sanae in a bad way?"

"They have a son."

"Really?"

"Yes, a nifty retarded or autistic or disabled son, named Denny."

"Graham never mentioned him to me."

"Nor to me," Moran said, realizing instantly she would take that as evidence of Moran's social ineptitude.

"Were you sleeping with him, too?" She asked, distantly laughing.

"Yes, I always wanted to have his son."

"It would take Japan's finest medical skill." She said, "Now why did you call?"

"I don't know. Graham thinks—"

"Thought," she corrected him.

"Graham believed Atcheson was murdered in the alleged plane crash—that's why the Army Air Force still refuses to provide the investigation's final report. Graham filed an appeal and threatened to sue."

"I knew that. Tell me something I didn't know. What was Graham's home life like?"

"They were on the verge of separating."

"That I didn't know. He said it would come years later."

"Sanae sees his death as liberation, but she really doesn't know where to go."

"And Denny?"

"A real problem if she comes back to Japan, as her brother wants."

"So you're going to save her?"

"I don't think so. I'd rather save you."

"You couldn't. You don't speak the language, and I'll bet you're a lousy swimmer."

"I do okay in very hot tub water."

"We can discuss it when you get back. Are you coming back?"

"I have classes."

"It would take the bureaucracy a full semester to figure out you weren't holding them."

"You don't want me to come back?"

"Mostly I want to know why you called."

"I wanted to hear an un-grieving, un-stoned voice. I wanted to luxuriate in the sound of clear priorities."

"Such a romantic. I do grieve for Graham, but we both knew what was going on and how it would eventually stop going on."

"What do you know about Green Cross?" Moran asked, running out of banter.

"The Japanese Red Cross, maybe. Started after the war by the pharmaceutical companies. A kind of nesting place for returning overseas Japanese doctors, guaranteeing them an income."

"Especially doctors from Unit 731?"

"I've heard that—shielding them from war crimes prosecution."

"Exactly. Yes exactly and that's what Atcheson found out and he was convinced if it became public that the U.S. government had struck a deal with Ishii. In return for his data, his doctors would be slotted back into Japanese life without any prosecution. He'd told the military, told MacArthur or told his Chief of staff, told Willoughby, he'd told everyone he could at headquarters about the deal, but he recognized they already knew about it, already sanctioned it. He alone was outraged. He was headed for Congress to lay it all out and stop the deal."

"Graham had sketched that out for me."

"And you never told me?"

"It was just speculation then. Graham liked to play with explanations . . . what he called scenarios. I assumed he'd have five more before he found the precise data to demonstrate the one he'd settled on. Besides I hardly shared everything Graham and I did, with you. Why would I?"

"Is Green Cross still functioning?"

"Yes, I think so. It's prestigious in fact. Maybe it's in every prefecture."

"And aboard every ferry," Moran said with some elation.

"Ah, you've caught the Guade disease."

"Ship screws didn't make those cuts."

"Is that why you called? To test a nutty theory?"

"I just wanted to hear your voice. It's late here—"

"I know that—noon day sun here . . . Now do you want to know why I was about to call you. Except of course I don't have your number."

"Why?"

"Do you know a Thomas Cole?"

"I know the name. Never met him. He has a copy of Atcheson's 123 File. He was ahead of me at Norton Air Force Base. I missed him by a day."

"He wants to get together with you at Livingston Wells' place in Sharon, Connecticut."

"He wants to or Wells wants to?"

"I don't know. You can sort it out. He said Secretary Wells wants to invite you to Sharon to discuss the Atcheson case. He said he some ideas about the case. And he'd be there in two days. He's driving up from Princeton."

"They both want to discuss the Atcheson accident?"

"Yes. Cole said he has ideas to clear up Hesseltine's translation notes."

"I bet. Did he have the address in Sharon?"

"143 Main Street. You should be able to find it."

"I wonder if he thinks I'm made of money and drive anywhere he wants."

"He did say Wells would reimburse you for a flight, if that was how you wanted to get there. You could fly into Hartford and drive from there."

"I bet. I'm supposed to eat this car?"

"If he calls back, what am I supposed to tell him?" Turid asked.

"What do you think?"

"Do what Graham would have done. Isn't that your motto now?"

"It didn't work out so well for Graham," Moran answered.

"Well, it solved a problem marriage and a lifetime responsibility for Denny. That's not a bad resolution, is it?"

"I like the way you get at the kernel of each day. Tell Cole I'll show up in Sharon in my trusty Pontiac. Maybe in two, probably three, days."

"David?" Turid said.

"Yes."

"Don't take the ferry."

Part VII, Wells' Triumph

"Ah Professor Moran, welcome to Great Elm and thanks so very much for taking a fling at my invitation."

"A fling?"

"Just an expression. Gratitude for being willing to drive so far just to hear State's side of the story, so to speak. My side and brother Cole's I suppose too, since he's been as active as you pursuing the truth of Graham's death and Atcheson's. Perhaps they were linked? What do you think?"

"I'm alert to every nuance," Moran said, smiling—happy that the expression seemed to derail Wells' bonhomie of welcome.

"Have you heard of Great Elm and the great, great doings here? Bill Buckley's a distant cousin of my Virginia—linked somehow to Priscilla. And in the ruling class there are always overlaps, don't you agree? So anyway, Bill always offers me the considerable hospitality of Great Elm whenever I need mountain air refreshment."

"I don't think much of the Berkshires as mountains," Moran said evenly, but it did not blur Wells' welcome.

"Well doubtless your western roots rule out thinking much of our soft hills, but in fact the perspective from our little rolling ones is quite remarkable. Later I'll walk you down to General Groves' place which has a really magnificent view of the valley farms stretching toward the northeast. His house is quite modest, but I suppose if you've built the Pentagon you already know from the inside what grandeur can achieve. Don't you agree?"

"I didn't know Groves lived here."

"Oh little Sharon shares its treasures with all kinds of prominent folks, not least of whom is Bill Buckley himself, as he has constantly reminds me—a small price to pay for these lovely digs to call my own since the Buckleys are seldom here. They have a better insulated place in South Carolina. Doubtless you are familiar with "The Sharon Statement," the proclamation that initiated Young Americans for Freedom. It's stipulation concerning the role of government is still my favorite brief summary of the American promise. I actually spent most of the happiest summers of my youth here in Sharon. I know every volume in the Sharon Hotchkiss library. Imagine, I first learned chess taking out books on the game and do you know for the first summer months of my 12th year I actually thought every game had only two opponents, Black and White. It never occurred to me to read the actual names of the player below the titles <u>Black</u> and <u>White</u>. I suppose Carlos has taken your bags to your room; it's upstairs, third door on the left."

"I <u>am</u> tired from the drive. I hadn't realized getting across upstate New York would be so long and desolate."

"I'm not so sure desolate is the right adjective for the empire state. You and I have been to far more desolate places, isn't that true? Even the Inland sea has its desolate moments, when the horizon is nothing but dank green water and a few island mounds swelling green against the suicidal, dark sky." Wells paused, studied Moran's blank face and then, "but enough sad thoughts. Carlos has hummus and chips, maybe some kind of cheese—probably too spicy—for you in the kitchen. He's a very accommodating fellow."

"You said Prof. Cole is here or not here? I didn't quite follow—probably too damn tired."

"Tom will get here tomorrow. He elected to stop off at friends in Westport on his way up from Princeton. I told him not to rush. He's done quite enough for me and for State."

"You sent him to California, to Norton?"

"Indeed. Once Graham discovered the missing 123 file, State took a hefty interest in looking at it. Bureaucracies don't like others knowing more about themselves than they know. It's a good rule of thumb. Absolutely mastery belongs to the actor, not the assessor. Don't you agree? Graham didn't, and paid some kind of price for his knowledge. Don't you agree? But we surely don't have to talk shop tonight. You deserve rest and deliverance from this old retired Foreign Service fool, who still believes in morality and destiny."

"Destiny?"

"America's task of leading the world toward that shining city on the hill," Wells said.

"Too tall an order for me."

"But not apparently for Graham, and that's perhaps the rub. Don't you agree?"

"Out of tiredness I agree, per force, with everything you say."

"I'm glad we're recording this," Wells said. "Now please go to bed upstairs."

Moran found that Carlos had placed his Delsey bag horizontally on the luggage rack at the end of the queen size, four poster bed. There was heft to the thick white quilt that squished down the lush green duvet topping the mattress. It seemed recent polyurethane had been applied thickly to the wide pine floor boards. For a family estate, the room appeared incongruously B & B in texture, gleaming cleanness and inviolability. A younger generation had already made crucial decisions concerning the manse's future. Moran felt appropriately transitional—the two night guest with academic credentials and limited income testing the Sharon receptivity and doubtless finding the place too tranquil and settled—a decorator's vision of New England's solidity and utterly tamed imagination. Would Turid have lasted a night in such stodginess? He couldn't summon her guiding him into the massive, iron footed tub easily deep enough for two. Instead he lay down in his clothes, yanking sleep like the duvet over him.

He awoke nine hours later to the smell of frying bacon—a scent he knew he'd rarely smell in Japan, or he reckoned in Southern California or Ohio either. For a delicious moment Moran remembered his experience as a 14 year old finding amid the breakfast buffet at a Sheraton Hotel, an immense stainless steel tray piled high with cooked bacon. He ate strip after strip and nothing else for a whole forty minutes of devouring. There could be no point of satiation and if now he could believe he had been so careless with his cholesterol count, then he believed he had tapped into the universe's final pleasure, out-notching even Turid. So Carlos was master chef as well?

But it was not Carlos doing the frying. Instead Moran found another fellow about his age adding rather thick bacon strips to the griddle section of the Great Elm's eight burner stove.

"They keep pigs at Great Elm, did you know that?" he said to Moran. "Do their own slaughtering and presto, you get these unbelievably thick lean slices. Surely the greatest bacon you or anyone else will have in this short life."

"Yes, and sure to shorten it even more," Moran responded.

Abruptly the fellow turned away from cooking, "I'm Tom Cole. Thanks so much for driving up to see us."

Moran latched on to the "us"—sorting through what sort of alliance, partnership Cole might have with Wells. The speculation was stayed as Cole said, "I've been Liv's researcher helping him write his memoirs, although things got off the tracks when Graham raised the issue of the 123 File."

"And that's what brought you to California?"

"Both Liv and State wanted a copy of everything in the file, since they never logged it."

"I think I missed you by a day."

"Liv wanted me back to continue our work on his book, and State wanted its copy, without having to request it directly. I offered to go. It more than fit my needs, since I'm writing a biography of Atcheson."

"Riveting work," Moran noted sourly, enjoying for the moment the strange look Cole gave him.

"Whatever. This is the best bacon this side of Chicago." Cole held out a piece for Moran.

"Bring in your plates. We might as well get started," Wells hollered from the long dining room. He was seated at the far end of twenty foot cherry table. Morning sunlight seemed to impregnate the glossy gleaming surface of the cherry panels parsing the table's length.

"Did Carlos slaughter the pig?" Moran asked sitting down four chairs away from Wells. Cole took the other side of the table.

Wells smiled broadly and said, "Carlos kills whatever I tell him to kill." He laughed. They all chuckled.

"You wanted to get started?" Moran continued.

"First, eat your blueberries," Wells said, pushing a mammoth cut class bowl toward Moran. "Powerful anti-oxidants."

"And Carlos didn't pick them," Cole said.

More mutual chuckles.

"I wanted to explain my memory lapse in Tokyo a while back, so I'm very appreciative that you'd come all this way to listen. Of course I could say that in one's 70's certain lapses are rather predictable. But I could tell you thought, as did Graham—he told me later—that I was prevaricating. Maybe I was. I'm not always clear on that issue. But I wanted you to know those were difficult times. Not because of Atcheson's troubles with Hurley but because of difficulties between State and SCAP, MacArthur's Headquarters, and because . . . because also of my own personal difficulties. Ginny and I were going through a difficult time. Not unknown among Foreign Service marriages. It was pretty clear MacArthur was not happy with any suggestion, much less interference on the part of the State Department, and George was exasperated that SCAP was calling all the shots concerning prosecution of war criminals, as well as designation of all 'legitimate' and acceptable Japanese politicians. Mac ran the whole show and he and Wilkinson didn't allow for dissent, or legal quibbles. But as Hurley well knew George didn't knuckle under to received wisdom, especially if that wisdom contradicted George's rather ornate and severe moral code."

"By 'ornate'" Cole said, "he means elaborate, over wrought, top heavy, many trellised."

"Like your clarification," Moran added.

Wells laughed. "I can see we'll have some fun sparring about these lamentable deaths, won't we? Don't you agree?"

"Just how pissed off was Atcheson?" Moran asked.

"Well, that was Graham's question," Wells answered. "And he thought George was outraged. I suspect when history is written, whatever that is, Graham Guade and George Atcheson will be seen as two peas in a pod. Both were utterly and absolutely convinced of their righteousness, their absolute grasp of actual truth and both destined to act accordingly out of such imperishable righteousness. Bless them both. Rest in peace, and thank God they're gone from the landscape. So the rest of us can sleep at night, and mind our business, tend our families and enjoy each sunset."

"The sunsets here are good but not in the class of those golden West Coast of Florida productions, with Cecile B. DeMille directing the cloud scape over the Gulf of Mexico." Cole said in a rush of enthusiasm.

"An entirely gratuitous comparison, Tom, unworthy of the gravity of this situation. Why is it, when historians think their narrative is dragging, invariably describe the weather? Do they imagine knowing the season and the temperature will galvanize their readers?" Wells said with some chastise-ment hidden in the smiling mirth.

Trying to pull things back on track, Moran said, "How bitter and vindictive was Atcheson toward SCAP and MacArthur?"

"Mean enough to get them indicted. Mean enough to get them imprisoned, or at least regarded as the moral blackguards they were—at least in his jaundiced eyes." Wells answered. "Mean enough to want to bring down the whole governing scaffolding SCAP represented in Japan."

"And how could he do that?" Moran asked.

"Graham didn't tell you?"

"Graham told me very little."

"About Unit 731? About Ishii's little hospital of horrors in Harbin?"

"I know about that now at least, but very little from Graham per se. Mostly from Turid and Hesseltine . . . maybe not the most reliable witnesses."

"Hehn!" Cole exclaimed, suggesting a knowledge of both which thoroughly surprised Moran.

"In fact Hesseltine on Unit 731 was too damning a witness, precisely the sort of fellow Atcheson would respond to and consequently be overwhelmed by, it seems to me. Don't you agree? Daily Archer kept pressing each astounding translation on Atcheson and asking what was being done to bring the butchers to justice? Ishii and company made Himmler and Mengele look like the Five Little Peppers. And somehow Ishii and his doctors avoided any round-up, any prosecution. It drove Hesseltine batty, and eventually Atcheson too. He sent missive after missive to SCAP, and when nothing happened, he copied State, then Congressmen. And then he threatened to go to the press with Archer's devastating elaborately recorded atrocities. Juicy stuff indeed—far juicier than what Atcheson had on Hurley, and it was pretty clear what kind of hornet's nest would be stirred up with such sheets."

Cole said, "And Graham pretty well understood what Atcheson was going through as he watched his attempts at exposure of 731 get stifled, first at SCAP, then at State, then in Congress. Important people had agreed to whatever deal Ishii had struck to save his own hide and the hides of his key doctors, who all got very good deals in post war Japan—really sweet deals, from the best preserved, least bombed out apartments, to heavily funded positions in Green Cross."

"Green Cross?" Moran said.

"Yes," Wells answered. "Japan's answer to the Red Cross—funded by the pharmaceutical firms and very much an on-going proposition."

"I think," Moran said, "Sanae Guade's brother Yasunari works for Green Cross."

"Bingo!" shouted Wells, laughing. "Everything fits together, don't you agree?"

"I'm not sure what you mean?"

"Don't be childish, David," Wells continued. "Green Cross might feel—what shall we say—inconvenienced, if an American diplomat in D.C. persuaded Congress to prosecute their senior officers as war criminals—perhaps even pursuing death penalties. Surely that might inhibit economic growth of the firm, don't you agree? Perhaps jeopardize the good will of the people for whom they ministered?"

"So Green Cross engineered the accident that happened to kill Atcheson?" Moran asked.

Wells answered, "Graham never jumped to conclusions. He just kept asking more and more embarrassing questions, raising more and more embarrassing scenarios. You had to admire and mightily resent his relentlessness—the kind of person you might employ and quickly grow to hate. Sooner or later you knew he'd turn on you no matter how helpful you had been to him. Do you see?"

"No."

"Well, who else might brother Atcheson, the righteous one, have threatened? Whose authority might he have challenged? Whose authority was considered absolutely sacrosanct in post war Japan?"

"SCAP and MacArthur, of course," Cole said.

"Oh, well done, my sunny researcher," Wells laughed. "Here's an irony Graham very much appreciated—Green Cross, the Japanese cover corporation, and SCAP the American, way-off-the-reservation Command Structure, both wanted hapless George out of the way. What could have been easier for them, in some kind of cooperative mode than to set George aside in the rich cool waters off Hawaii? What could have been easier? Don't you agree?"

"I don't see how you'd engineer a plane accident that kills only a few of the passengers," Moran said. "Suppose you took out the wrong ones? And why invite a sure-fire and very thorough investigation?"

"Ah," Wells said, "you sound like Graham more and more each day we spend together—"

"We haven't spent any days together."

"Is that regret I hear in your tone?"

"Well, you do seem to find first rate accommodations."

"Bill Buckley, despite a somewhat prickly personality, always lived well. But Graham was bothered precisely by your question, and that was leading him in new directions. Perhaps closer to more lethal enemies. But why don't we take a break here, a little sporting hiatus. I can get my morning nap. And we can resume over lunch." Wells smiled paternally and indicated by getting up that his proposal was not open to negotiation. "Tom get Carlos to drive you and David out to Cream Hill Pond for a little swim. It's delicious there."

2.

Against all reason Moran heard something like a threat in Wells' directive to Cole, and the inclusion of Carlos only added to Moran's anxiety. So much so that on the drive to the pond he asked the swarthy valet/driver the inevitable question: "Carlos, have you ever been to Japan?" Nor was Moran's nervousness much assuaged by the Filipino's quiet answer: "Many times."

Many times played over in Moran's head. The phrases cast a new light on Carlos. It now seemed he was not some Buckley family retainer, employed to watch over the estate's transition, but more ominously a confidant or henchman of Wells. It was patently absurd the notion spinning in Moran's mind that Carlos might be a murderous minion of the suave Assistant Secretary, but there was a kind of humorous glamor in summoning such a vision. Would he swerve the car into a thick oak tree in such a way the passenger in the back seat would be terminated? And would Moran be listed in the black book of execution right below Guade's name? And would Moran's accidental "embarkment" be a discussion point at the terminal ninth hole of the Sharon Country Club?

Moran's obsession convinced him not to climb into the long yellow canoe Carlos and Cole used to drift into the center of the small pond. The edge of the water reflected a myriad whispering popular tree bristling, clinking leaves, and Moran sat on a thick brown towel on the one sandy beach watching the canoe and pretending to read his paperback copy of Walker Percy's *The Moviegoer*. But Moran couldn't keep from imagining Carlos and Guade at the stern of the ferry on the still, dark Seto Inland Sea. Doubtless Guade probing Carlos for information about Wells' dealings with Atcheson, and then looking deep into the Filipino's eyes, Guade realizing at the last moment Carlos was not a gentle factotum of the great man's but rather his enforcer in that last amazed moment (two quick knife swipes) before he was pushed into the churning waters. Ridiculous, of course, Moran realized but surely more delicious than Wells' assertion about Cream Hill Pond. Even now Moran theorized Carlos knocking the hapless Cole over the side and in the epic emptiness and silence of the solitary pond, watched as Cole flailed about, and then systematically the Filipino began clubbing Cole with his paddle—each strike opening blood streams into the dark waters, thin streams downward among the upward weeds whitening as they sought the light above. Instead, both men paddled slowly back to Moran's tiny beach. Before they reached him Cole flipped into the water and shouted how bracing it was in the soft summer air.

On the drive back Moran felt sheepish and neurotic for fantasizing canoe brutality, then strangely comic for fashioning such foolishness. He regretted not swimming himself. But back at the long cherry table Wells summoned him again to apparently the historian's task—explicating the past.

"So we've established that both the Japanese and the U.S. army structures might have had cause to seek brother Atcheson's removal." Wells said. "But aren't we letting ourselves off the hook."

Moran immediately said, "I am not now, nor have I ever been, a member of the 'Atcheson must die' organization."

"So you are truly exempt," Wells laughed. "But we must remember that SCAP did not instigate the salvation of Ishii's organization. That gift emanated from another branch of the government—State Department surely, but also the OSS, and what the Secretary would eventually call 'the primitives' in Congress who wanted to make sure the U.S. held all the cards of mass destruction. Wanted desperately to make sure America led in biological-chemical warfare—led definitively. For such 'primitives' Ishii would prove the ultimate source and icon, the jewel in the crown of atrocity. And anyone who threatened that jewel, either through direct action or public exposure would have to be eliminated. Have I made the case, brother Cole?"

"Aye, aye, Captain!" Cole nearly whispered, cocking his head.

"And thus having made the case we should add the whole U.S. government as possible enemies of Atcheson. Enemies enough to take direct action. Don't you agree?"

"I agree," Cole said.

"But the evidence for an accident is overwhelming," Moran said.

"And that Graham seemed to endorse, but only after meticulous review of the plane's record. And it was the refusal of the Air Force to release the final report on the flight that fired up Prof. Guade in the first place. Yes, he determined there were some anomalies in the preliminary investigation. When the flight left Kwajalein the record indicated there was enough fuel for an eight hour flight. But the flight to Oahu should have taken only four hours. Yet the plane ditched because fuel was spent. Graham discovered in the preliminary records that some technician speculated the B-17 had a 'fuel burner' engine on one side. Such phenomena were not unknown for that bomber. Good enough for Guade, the indefatigable. Good enough for me," Wells said. "But there was the mysterious extra passenger at Kwajalein, Captain Sigmond who apparently perished in the ditching, as did George Atcheson. Who was Sigmond, and why did he just board the flight? Guade was investigating those questions. He told me he was fascinated by them, since the Army had many records of many Captain Sigmonds but none at Kwajalein at that particular time. No one had checked for Navy records of him or Army Air Force ones. More interesting for Guade was the appearance of a U.S. Coast Guard rescue ship, *Hermes* at the very position the B-17 went into the sea. A fortunate turn of events for the three survivors. And Graham the formidable researcher, managed to wheedle out of the Pentagon the transcripts from that ship to various authorities overseeing the disaster."

"But he never saw those transcripts," Cole said loudly. "I've seen them. I got them or a copy of them from Petelchuk and there's a further discrepancy. Captain Sigmond joined at Kwajalein, and before that at Haneda in Japan, Captain

Peterson also joined. The original orders listed Atcheson and four others as passengers but noted that up to two more could be added by the Chief of Staff. Counting Peterson and Sigmond there were 14 people on the flight, but the official record notes only 13. Three survived with injuries, five bodies were recovered—one was alive for a while but died. And five or maybe six were never recovered, including Atcheson. I don't think Graham ever got around to checking on Peterson. Sigmond was inexplicable enough, maybe."

"Perhaps we're losing the thread," Wells said. "The important thing is that something strange was going on vis a vis the flight itself, and in a couple of scenarios Graham discussed with me, he theorized that perhaps SCAP did not want to see its prerogative of overseeing everything in occupied Japan be whisked away to some Congressional investigation or to some other Executive entity and therefore SCAP might have wished for Atcheson's removal. And Graham theorized SCAP might have joined forces with other U.S. agencies who wished to keep under wraps the rather sickening moral bargain they had made with Ishii and Unit 731 doctors to carry off their findings and data in toto in return for no prosecution for war crimes. Only the *maruta* once again were violated by such an agreement with hell. Graham wondered if MacArthur and the gang at Fort Dietrich, the bio warfare group in Maryland, joined hands to bring the B-17 down."

"That's ridiculous—how would they do it? Hire a saboteur to damage the wing engines to guarantee descent near a rescue ship? Absurd." Moran said.

"Nonsense," Wells objected. "O.S.S. cut their teeth on such operations. But more importantly, Graham overlooked a much more likely, more effective actor. One he should have been aware of since he had only to look at his own extended family."

"What are you talking about?" Cole asked.

"Tom, I'm talking about something you should have tripped on by now. Graham surely would have. I'm talking about Green Cross. I'm talking about Graham's wife's brother, and all the now elderly doctors from Unit 731—doctors that Green Cross sheltered."

"I don't understand," Moran said wearily.

"You don't understand the reverence Ishii is held in, the reverence, the worship, his name induces. His atrocities made him legendary in Japan's supreme war effort. From the start he was regarded, and still is regarded, as a scientist and innovator beyond human capacities. A genius at advancing Japan's interests, a sponsor of a thousand young geniuses, who advanced the science of mass killing beyond the wildest imaginings of the sickest German butchers. Outstripped them all and withal the most humble of human beings, the quintessential Japanese—self-effacing, compliant, yet God-like. Supremely worthy of adulation even as he knelt offering himself tirelessly to the Empire of Japan. Think Gandhi subsumed into Joe DiMaggio wrapped in Isaac Newton."

"I get the picture."

"Get the fuller picture of his adulators and what they might be capable of, if sent even the subtlest signal of direct action. You are familiar, aren't you with the term 'direct action' in Japanese history."

"I grasp assassination."

"One phrase and forty volunteers to perish with George Atcheson. One hundred volunteers to shove poor Graham Guade off the end of the ferry. A thousand anxious to sword swipe Graham Guade. And how many waiting in the wings to do in old David Moran for taking up Graham's mantle?"

Moran interiorly wondered if that were a direct threat, but only said. "And they'd be so well placed as to join the flight with Ambassador Atcheson without exciting interest before or after the butchery? I'm not buying it. It might have been more plausible for one fanatic to join the ferry to Hiroshima, I suppose. But even that pushes the envelope. Who could have known Graham was going for moonlit frolic on Seto Inland Sea. Only, I suppose, someone accompanying him. Tell me Liv was Carlos with you on the ferry?"

"Don't be absurd."

"I'm just illustrating a point—the whole argument is absurd."

"Defending Japan's honor is hardly absurd. I can tell you that. But of course you already know it."

"It's true," Cole said, "I gave a guest lecture at Handai once suggesting that the atomic bomb had little to do with ending the war, and I got roundly accused of missing the whole point. 'We would never have been defeated, except for the accident of your technology. You could never have defeated us.' That rang out like a chorus from a class that ordinarily was terrified to speak any English. It amazed me."

"There," Wells shouted, "See how brilliant young Cole is. How wise despite his years." Wells laughed. "But he brings up the fundamental point—namely accident. What does the conscientious historian do with accident? Maybe Graham simply lost his balance—he sure as hell did you know—historically. Maybe Atcheson's plane lost an engine because a screw broke loose somewhere. I like those ideas, those interpretations."

"A screw broke loose here, that's for sure," Moran added. "Two deaths separated by what? Thirty two years. But, fascinatingly, each death threatened precisely the same groups. Despite thirty two years passing, the same groups felt existentially threatened, and the same eventuality played out.

The threat-makers died quickly, dramatically, extinguishing the threat."

"And so we come to the nub of the discussion," Wells said, pouring himself what looked to be port from a large etched glass decanter. Do we have threat-makers here to carry on George and Graham's tireless work? Do we?"

"And you're implying it's more than academic question. Do you agree?" Moran said with a not hidden mockery in his tone.

"I wonder what you could be thinking, David. Do you think of me as an initiator of anything? Really?"

"Of course not," Moran answered, "you're a kindly, re-tired old viper—a would-be Sicilian on a borrowed estate."

"Careful!" Wells laughed and cautioned.

"Besides," Moran continued, "we've overlooked the clearest, direct explanation. Sanae told me her brother, Yasu-nari killed Graham."

"Absolutely astonishing!" Wells shouted. "Bravo! All we have to do is established that he, what was his name?"

"Yasunari."

"Yes, all we have to do is establish that Yasunari was actually on the ferry with Graham. But, alas, the ferry never keeps list of passengers. You buy a ticket and you yield it up and you, like the ticket, get tossed away . . . "

Cole said, "I didn't know Sanae Graham had a brother."

"Or a little boy, a little autistic boy named Denny. I bet you didn't know that either, Tom." Moran said. "Actually Sanae only said Yasunari saved her by showing her she didn't have to stay with Graham. She could come back to Japan. Yasunari would help her. But of course she wouldn't go back there."

"Why not?" Cole asked.

"For obvious reasons," Wells said. "A Japanese woman scarred with western ways and burdened with a disabled child. Obviously she wouldn't go back to Japan. And that's not the point. The point is as follows: Maybe SCAP could have killed George but SCAP wasn't around to kill Graham; maybe Green Cross was around at both times to terminate George and Graham; and maybe the U.S. agencies involved killed George and Graham—they're still around. Maybe Yasunari killed Graham but was hardly around to kill George. Or maybe accidents iced both victims. Sorting all that out is a nifty game, worth two or three decanters of whatever Buckley left for us here." Wells pointed to the etchings on the glass. "But that's just a game. What's not a game is who's left playing? Do we have a player to take up Graham's cause, and if we do, what do we do to protect him from George and Graham's fate? Or is it simply a matter of convincing him that taking up the burden is not worth the possible snuffing of the candle?"

"You don't have to convince me. It was only a lark on my part from the start. Hardly worth even another moment of inquiry," Moran said.

"But I'm doing a book on George Atcheson," Cole said.

"Ah, your little text. A model monograph that needs only to dismiss as stupid speculation any reference to what we've been laying on the table."

"On pain of death," Moran added laughing.

"Whose death?" Cole asked, apparently genuinely puzzled.

"Your death, Tom," Wells answered laughing louder.

"Why my death?" Cole asked.

"You'd best ask that of David, here. He knows how careers are made, and what the parameters are." Wells said. "He'll be your mentor. You can't go wrong."

"I can't go wrong," Cole echoed.

"History depends on evidence," Wells said. "And in the absence of evidence the wise historian is silent. Isn't that so, David?"

"Oh, absolutely," Moran said.

"Absolutely," Wells said, looking at Cole.

"Absolutely," Cole concurred. "I can show the mindlessness of such speculations in my biography of Atcheson."

"Good thinking, lad," Wells said. "We'll look forward to your tome. Won't we, David?"

"Oh, absolutely."

"And if, David, you can avoid despair, you'll surely be able to guide Tom on his inquiry, safe guarding history's integrity, won't you?"

"Oh, absolutely."

"In fact I'd like to aid you, Tom, in completing your biography of Atcheson by relieving you of your research chores for my paltry memoir. David I'd like to put you on as the chief writer, the one most able to encompass and encapsulate Tom's wonderful preliminary spade work. And, Tom, just to let you know that I always put my money where my mouth is, please tell your Department Chair that I'll pick up whatever expense there might be in hiring an adjunct to teach your courses for the next semesters so you can focus on completing your book. Now, how's that for our own little Sharon Statement?"

"The embodiment of the American promise," Cole said loudly.

"Oh, absolutely," Moran said.

Epilogue, 2016

"You are perhaps wondering what happened to Professor Moran, and in fact I can't really say, since I don't know. What I do know is that I got a last minute telephone call saying Moran would not be available, and asking if could I fill in, since my evaluations for previous lectures had been, —and here's the key phrase—'rather favorable.' Yes, I spoke on this cruise a few years back and, I'm a 'rather favorable' kind of guy, having written a long time ago a 'rather favorably reviewed' book on George Atcheson, one of the U.S's lamentable 'China Hands' during a good portion of World War II. Anyway I agreed, on really astounding short notice, to fill in for Moran, whose credentials, I acknowledge, are far more impressive than my own. So let's get it right out on the table: you're going to be disappointed. Life is disappointment. If you can push past that disappointment I contend you'll still learn a lot about China and Southeast Asia on this cruise from my lame lectures. Also you'll get information about perhaps the most successful Asian leader of the 20th century, Lee Kuan Yew.

"But I'm no Moran, just a solid, pale shadow of his expertise. It's a shame he isn't here to fulfill his part of the contract you made for this cruise. Is his absence enough for you to get a discount or rebate on your ticket? Maybe so. It's surely worth a try, just don't link my advice and name with your attempt." He paused for a laugh, but none came. "So I'm Thomas Cole, last minute—called at the last minute—substitute lecturer, over the hill and under the radar, imitation expert, faux wise man, available always on the shortest notice possible, mildly enthusiastic under-study not quite ready for prime time, but tossed in just the same. At the end of the day, I'm the low-hanging fruit of academic life, gathered just before spoilage, on the verge of plopping onto the earth for re-absorption. You get the picture."

A hand went up in the back of the 25 or so attendees at this initial lecture. "Do you have a question?"

"Yes, I have a question. Yes I do."

"Please go ahead."

"I have a question, and my question is, are you a Christian?"

"I don't see the relevance of that."

"Where we're going I suspect there are very few Christians, so I think it's relevant to know if we're being instructed by a Christian. And this is supposed to be a Christian cruise."

"I doubt that. Deny that. This is a non-denominational cruise. I suspect we have many non-Christians aboard, don't we? Muslims perhaps, surely some Buddhists, maybe a Hindu or two . . . Shintoists, atheists, what have you."

"I was told this was a Christian Cruise."

"Good Christians I suspect don't take cruises. They give to the poor. And there are no poor here," drawing a mild audience chuckle.

"Very funny, but I'm still waiting for your answer."

"Your question doesn't deserve an answer, but just for the record I stopped being a Christian shortly after my 16th birthday. I'm closer to atheistic Buddhism than anything

I suspect. As was the fellow I came here to talk about. Lee Kuan Yew—surely one of the greatest figures of the twentieth century and very probably an atheist, near-Buddhist like me. Since we're just leaving Singapore, let me get started on Singapore's greatest genius, the only successful utopian politician, in the sense he actually created a utopia—the only one in the history of humankind from Noah to this very precious moment now at 8:22 p.m.," Cole checked his watch, "aboard the Empress of the Seas."

"Okay. Okay. Lee was Mr. Wonderful, top drawer. One of the best. Indeed a genius, but also a secular punk and this was billed as a Christian Cruise, and I for one came aboard because I wanted my faith renewed and I wanted to hear the Word of God spoken by people who had spent their life listening to Christian music and thinking Christian thoughts. You don't show me much."

"Are you drunk?"

"Fucking A! I'm drunk, drunk on the rescue from your bilge of meaningless living, accumulating tidbits of possessiveness and consumption and emptiness and empty, empty emptiness."

"Perhaps it would be better if you just simply left."

And the fellow did so—an impressive exit, turning his tall back on the audience and very slowly walking toward the right back door of the large grey-painted room, his dark green canvas traveler's jacket (festooned with wide flapless pockets) swinging a bit as he moved. It seemed his red, buzz cut hair gleamed through the fluorescent light at the exit. The sound of the ship's screws cutting the sea came through the slow opening door.

2.

"I didn't think this was a Christian Cruise—whatever that means," she said as Cole came to stand beside her at the railing. Below the sea now was glassy quiet, barely intersected by the ship's edge. For a moment he thought about flinging himself over the stantions. He wondered if his body would shatter the sea surface. He imagined he would detonate into a fine quartz faience. Would she toss him a life ring? There were three along the railing, all within easy reach. On the other hand she was clearly elderly, (as were all the others on board) and not up to tossing life rings, or any weighty objects for that matter. Her face was heavily rouged, doubtless applied over a layer or two of primer, to smooth over the age spots and wrinkles that he himself had come to watch in the extension circular shaving mirror that he always pulled too close to his cheek, as if to receive life-directions directly through the blue/white gel foam that inevitably touched the glass.

"I've noticed the ship slows down when passengers need to walk the decks after dinner, after immortal lectures. In fact, they've cut the engines. " Cole said. "Did you enjoy my talk?"

"Not particularly. You have a way of droning on. It tends to put people to sleep."

"I appreciate your candor."

"I don't think you do, despite what you say. I don't particularly care, but I do acknowledge that you put some time into your lecture, and should be thanked for that. And God knows I didn't know anything about Lee Kuan Yew, or whatever."

Cole picked at the heavily varnished railing. He could push hard against it, confident it would not give way. He thought— first a Christian nut, and now a Candor nut. "I'm Tom Cole, formerly quite exciting on the topics of Asian history and culture."

She turned to him flashing a smile so wide it revealed cracks in her makeup around the corners of her mouth. "You can call me 'Widow Phillips'"

"I'm sorry to hear that."

"Don't be. In an hour or two come down to G Deck, Suite 1713, and perhaps we can alleviate your loneliness. There's always a soiree of attractive people, including younger crew members in my suite in the later evening. My daughter Evelyn invariably screws one or two of the Filipinos. You can watch or participate. You'll find relief from the monotony of these cruises. You're definitely invited— someone of robust build and sharply marked character."

Cole's involuntary laugh got short-circuited by the intense imploring of her stare into his eyes. "Let me ponder that a while."

"Don't ponder too long. Opportunity never lingers," she said, smiling and touching his forearm, then holding it for just too long a time.

"I thought this was a Christian Cruise." Cole said.

"We'll show you it's not," she said, smiling. "Even your blessed Lee Kuan Yew would have been interested. But he wouldn't have known about repentance and absolution."

"I don't think he would have been interested."

"His loss and yours. G Deck, suite 1713. Tootle loo!" and she hurried away.

3.

Wi-Fi from the ship was notoriously intermittent. He imagined not knowing her first name would make a standard

Google search fruitless. And he was discouraged that he could not even get to a full listing of the passengers. With despair he tried "Widow Phillips" but that yielded a Facebook entry about, apparently, a dog—a cur with Hispanic friends, and then next, the luscious blond widow of David Phillips, a British constable killed in Merseyside, England. She looked at least 50 years younger than the widow Phillips of Cole's swelling interest. So he poured himself a very long B & B, and after some calculation swallowed a Blue Diamond Viagra, then pocketed a second one. What if sylvan Evelyn turned out to be a svelter, smoother rendition of her mother?

Weren't cruises the most deliberate of all liaison activity? Weren't they created to bring love bristling out of improbable places and pairings?

Could the Widow Phillips actually be the Rubenesque courtesan of his furtive imaginings? Could he now at age seventy-one find fulfillment of those stifled dreams of his 17th year, a thousand summers ago? Would slight sadism figure in the brew? Stiletto heels driven deep into his back as she jumped and wiggled toward ultimate release from loin longing? He took another long swallow from his B&B and fingered several of his notecards of Lee Kuan Yew's wisest observations. Another swallow of the sweet, thick liquor as he read to himself: "There is a dearth of entrepreneurial talent in Singapore. We have to start experimenting. The easy things—just getting a blank mind to take in knowledge and become trainable—we have done. Now comes the difficult part. To get literate and numerate minds to be more innovative, to be more productive, is not easy. It requires a mindset change, a different set of values."

She held, obviously, a different set of values and here he was the literate, numerate, novice embarking on a mindset change. The prospect of it set him wobbling on the stairs up to G Deck, that summit of consumption—panoramic windows in all the Suites, and doubtless Tempur-pedic king-size mattresses, littered with pliant, obedient Filipino crew members.

But they weren't Filipinos—rather it was a middle-aged apparently Vietnamese couple, the man in a chef's hat and kitchen garb and the woman in grey sweatpants and a lavender sweater. They were seated on the couch, widow Phillips between them and reading a small thin picture book.

"Ah, Professor Cole, I knew you'd come," she smiled insanely, apparently congratulating herself. "I just knew it. I knew how to ask. I could tell the minute you began your lecture. And I so desperately need native speakers to help me in these lessons. Come, sit on the couch with us. There's plenty of room. And just read slowly each page's caption. Slowly. That's the important thing. The Nguyen's need to connect the sound of your voice with the picture they see. It helps if you can point to whatever you're saying." She held out the book.

He squeezed into the left end of the couch, pressing against the chef and taking the booklet, turned a page and slowly said, *"Max, the steam shovel, knew just what to do."*

"Point to the shovel," she directed.

He did so.

"Now pass the book back to me."

He did so.

"And that very night," she said slowly and too loudly, *"Max dug out the whole foundation . . .* That's a hard word, *foundation.* I bet you don't know what that word is, do you?"

The chef shook his head.

"Perhaps he knows *bondage,*" Cole said.

"Oh, I don't think so. He's actually a moral chef, maybe the only true moralist on this ship."

"I'm glad he's not deceptive," Cole said slowly, as she passed the booklet back to him. "*But suddenly Max realized he couldn't get out of the pit he had dug.*" He passed the text back to her. "Time to call Lee Kuan Yew, the ultimate fixer."

"Let's leave Lee out of this. I can see I owe you an apology for asking you here under, what shall we say, 'false circumstances'. It's just that I can't get native speakers of English on these cruises to help me at all. And, frankly, my livelihood depends on teaching successfully. It's something of a card house. The captain recruits the chef and helpers for nominal wages with the promise of free English lessons. And at the same time he offers me free accommodation so long as I can keep teaching these recruits. If we fail anywhere, we all perish."

"So what do I get for joining the game?"

"We can negotiate that, perhaps at some later and more opportune time."

"Doubtless after the cruise is over and I have nothing to bargain."

"You may not have much to bargain anyway. So few of us do," she said smiling.

"And, of course, there's no daughter Evelyn."

"Oh, there is. She lives in Pasadena—teaches third grade there. So she comes by it honestly."

"I wonder what 'it' refers to?"

"Whatever you'd like. I was thinking of teaching people to read English."

"I'd taken a pill for something else."

"That's sweet, really endearing, almost touching. But ultimately just silly."

It was clear the Nguyen's did not follow the conversation. They smiled too broadly.

"Time's up," she said firmly and slowly enough for the Nguyens to understand. "We have a new word to add to our collection. Not only **steam shovel** and **dig out** but also **foundation**. Please say it, **foundation**."

"**Fuh on day shun**," the Nguyens said.

4.

"We can see in the courtship and marriage of Lee Kuan Yew and the woman he always called 'Choo' one of the great love stories in history. If we go through it carefully we can find early evidence of Lee's incredible focus and commitment, his absolutely legendary tenacity in pursuing his lady love, and later his fierce conviction to tend to his beloved Singapore's independence and glowing future."

Cole noticed his audience was less and less attentive, drifting toward glazed eyes as he recited Lee's life as a Malaysian student at Cambridge, England, his complicated efforts to get Choo to join him in England, and eventually the "first" they both collected from their Colonial educational masters. Attention seemed to pick up as Cole presented Lee's conflict with the Special Branch from Singapore that in London tracked his interactions with groups thought to be Communist or at least disloyal to Britain. The paunchy elderly men of the audience did seem to brighten when Cole recited Lee's disillusionment with Britain's new Labour Government's turn toward egalitarianism and National Health Care. He read Lee's careful statement, so reflective of Lee's approach in Singapore years later:

"I was too young, too idealistic to realize that the cost to the government would be heavy, worse, that under such an egalitarian system each individual would be more interested in what he could get out of the common pool than in striving to do better for himself, which had been the driving force for progress throughout human evolution. That realization had to wait until the 1960s, when I was in charge of the government of a tiny Singapore much poorer than Britain, and was confronted with the need to generate revenue and create wealth before I could even think, let alone talk, of redistributing it."

Suddenly a hand went up again in the back. The red-haired fellow. "Redistribution is a Christian imperative, isn't it? Could you talk more about that?"

"I was just illustrating Lee's basic conservatism. Nothing more. Certainly nothing religiously. He wasn't a Christian."

"Why wasn't he, since you admire him so?"

"I'm not sure I see the correlation."

"You're not sure. You're not sure. You're not sure. Sure, you're not sure. How could you be? You couldn't be and you're not. Surely you're not."

"Let's get back to Lee Kuan Yew. His brilliant training in the law suddenly tossed him into Singaporean politics when unions came to him and asked him to represent their interests before a stiffening Colonial government. Soon enough he had made a reputation as an articulate advocate for local rights. It would only be a short walk to thinking seriously about independence. The British Empire was everywhere in collapse. The Japanese co-prosperity sphere had triggered profound change in the whole pacific basin. And it was clear Malaya would get independence from the Dutch, as would Singapore and Northern Borneo. Indeed the whole Straits Grouping would get its independence, but could it be linked together in a new configuration, in a new nation? That was the question, and Lee pursued—"

"I want to talk about redistribution. It's a very Christian substantive question. It's what I want to talk about." The red-haired fellow was standing up in the back again, but his resonant voice easily carried forward. Several listeners turned around to watch him.

In a way that seemed later, when Cole thought about it, almost providential Cole didn't directly confront the statement. Instead he took steps toward the fellow, and almost shouted: "Here's a better idea. Right after this lecture why don't you follow me to Widow Phillips suite G Deck 1713, and we can all talk about Christian redistribution while the widow teaches English as a second language to various members of this ship's crew. Isn't that a Jim-Dandy idea! What could be better? You get to do your desperate proselytizing, and I get to finish my immortal lecture for these infinitely patient and kind and slightly narcoleptic folks here. The crews learns English and we all get to understand who we are."

"I'm sure who I am."

"Splendid, meet you later on G Deck and we can sort it all out. I'll get to witness your light."

"I'm Archer Hesseltine, Presbyterian missioner, retired, resident now of The Pilgrim's Way, San Francisco, late loss of his own beloved Choo, Jena. Bereaved. Lonely. Numb feet. Weak knees, scraping hip joints, sometimes incontinent, short of breath, hard of hearing, cataract-ridden, ready for the short slide into the infinite oven of rest. I've been told a place for me in our father's house has been readied, but presently it's only a single room with cable and an adjacent entirely plastic bath capsule, imported from Japan. The sink faucet can be spun to the side to fill the tiny tub, or clamped with the sprinkler knob . . . 'Rainwater effect,' they call it. The whole unit has a single drain in the floor by the toilet. You can spray everywhere, to your heart's content."

"G Deck, in an hour." Cole said holding up his hand.

"I can't be summoned like some steward's mate."

"Not summons, only opportunity. Isn't that right, Widow Phillips?"

"I'm past all opportunity. You should be alert to that. You need to think about that. Opportunity is a synonym for death." And, green jacket flopping, he exited again.

5.

"There are no synonyms for death," Widow Phillips said at the next late evening ESL session. "And Archer surely knew that. He's such an impetuous fellow. But we mustn't neglect the Nguyens whose time, after all, is very limited. So perhaps you can begin, Professor, with Goodnight Moon."

"I'm familiar with it," Cole answered, "but don't you think it's a bit jejune for the Nguyens?"

"Evelyn loved it. Just read it and point to the pictures."

"Ah, Evelyn. Of course she would have liked it. **In the great green room There was a telephone And a red balloon And a picture of—**" Cole pointed to the green walls, the telephone on the nightstand, the floating balloon, and the picture above the fireplace. He repeated **room, telephone, balloon and picture.** But Mrs. Nguyen seemed sleepy and the chef had turned away. He shifted his position unhappily, stretched out his legs.

Cole said, "Maybe this story induces narcolepsy. Are you sleepy Mr. Nguyen?"

"Me sleepy. Me sleepy. She sleepy." The chef smiled.

"So there you have it," Cole said. "Seems we need a more lively story. Why don't you find one?"

"Ah, professorial to the end." Widow Phillips answered, and produced another slender, frayed booklet. "**The Large and Growly Bear . . . Once there was a large and growly**

bear. One spring morning, he woke up with nothing to do."

Cole echoed, "Yes, nothing to do. Not even a cruise to take. Mr. Nguyen, do you understand **'growly'?**"

"Glowly?" Mr. Nguyen answered.

"Not glowly but **growly**. Note the **grr** sound. **G.R. Growly**. Prof. Cole will growl for you, it's a bear sound. Growl, Professor, growl, as if still teaching undergraduates."

But before Cole could do so, or refuse to do so, the clamp to the Suite door flipped and Archer Hesseltine stepped into the crowded room. Widow Phillips passed the book to Cole, who glanced at the text but said nothing. Instead he thought, 'here is our bear.'

"I see no one yet is 'au naturel'—more evidence of that this is a Christian cruise, even though Buddhist Nha Trang is our next stop." Archer said, in a voice to wake Mrs. Nguyen. "So you weren't lying to me. This truly is an English lesson, not the 'English lesson' I was led to believe. No one abused, flagellated—no panting after being hurt. No reason for elderly thrill seekers to come through the door."

"Only to help stamp out illiteracy," Widow Phillips said. "Only to help those less fortunate in this life."

"Precisely as our savior stipulated."

"Your savior," Cole corrected.

"Ah, the unbeliever." Archer said, picking up the book and reading loudly: "**So the large and growly bear went growling, and prowling and scowling, looking for someone to frighten. And what did he see?**" Archer handed the book to Mr. Nguyen. "And what did he see? Indeed, what did he see? He saw bell jars full of malformed fetuses— babies without feet or eyes or noses, empty whitish forms pressed against the glass, through formaldehyde—rows and rows of them, ten rows high in warehouses, bell jars staring noiselessly out at old Professor Cole from America. Professor Cole on his way to Nha Trang. Innocent old Cole from America which had spread the soft mist of malformed fetuses all over the land to which old Cole now anticipated with such weaselly joy. Is it remembrance or combat envy that puts you in Nha Trang?"

"During that great effort I defended Staten Island, and Virginia Beach in the Coast Guard." Cole said.

"Heroic," Archer answered. "Heroic. Doubtless leading to a free graduate degree?"

Taking up the book Widow Phillips read: "**Sssh!' said the moles. 'You will shake the tunnels to China!' 'But I mean it', said the large and growly bear. 'I am frightening you!'**"

"What Sssh!?" Chef Nguyen said.

"**Sssh!** is very close to **Duh!...**" Archer said.

"That's not helpful," Widow Phillips said. "That's not helpful at all."

"My daughter knows **Duh!**" the Chef said with startling clarity.

6.

"Lee Kuan Yew surely understood violence and warfare. His rather vivid account of the Japanese takeover of Malaya in the Great War is ample proof he understood what atrocity was, and what kind of response atrocity required. And he surely knew about the atrocity the Indonesian government was committing against Lee's brethren Chinese in that country. And he gave every indication of grasping what threats were likely against his new country of Singapore. It's not a mistake that he supported U.S. efforts in Vietnam, and U.S. naval presence in the South China Sea. He guessed how essential that presence would be to prevent outside forces from gobbling up the utopia he was establishing."

Archer's hand shot upward from the back of the narrow room.

"I see Mr. Hesseltine you have yet another question. Please labor on."

"Not so much a question as a comment. In Japan where I lived for so very long I noticed at academic conferences the Japanese preferred to make long commentaries on whatever they had thought about during the foreign presentation, and at the end rather than a question they'd simply say, 'Would you comment on what I just said.' So in that spirit I should like to point out that American atrocity forced upon the Vietnamese people perhaps a million still-born births of the most grotesque kinds, and that those effects from the so called 'defoliation campaigns' continue to this very moment, since dioxin lingers in the soil for generations. And hence also in the ground water, and the eaten vegetables. What did your blessed Lee Kuan Yew say about that? I see nothing in his memoirs —certainly nothing in his first volume, anyway. And since this is a Christian cruise, please put a Christian spin on your words."

"This is not a Christian cruise. I think there is nothing in the cruise literature, in any of the cruise brochures that indicates this is a Christian cruise. So there's no need for me, or anyone, to 'spin' a Christian message during these lectures. I'm afraid you'll simply have to accept that fact. It is a fact. Having said that so I take it your real question is about Lee's apparent support for America in Vietnam. I only said he spoke out against the extent of American involvement, not the fact of that involvement, which he supported. Lee was no Christian pacifist. He perfectly understood the use of force—the absolute necessity of it. Here is a statement on that issue from the first volume, since you seem to like referencing it: 'As a result I have never believed those who advocate a soft approach to crime and punishment, claiming that punishment does not reduce crime. That was not my experience in Singapore before the war, during the Japanese occupation or subsequently.'

"So Lee, like all Americans, enjoyed beating people, inflicting pain and punishment and defoliation. Like all Americans he was a savage at heart and therefore to be envied, emulated, exalted. Why don't we put his face on all those bell jars of malformed fetuses festooning the museums and hospitals of Nha Trang? Or maybe only the ones in Ho Chi Minh City. Maybe he would have smiled on that, enthused about that, delighted in that. Would he?"

"Have a little Dukkha Mr. Hesseltine. Have a little Dukkha . . . It's inevitable as Mr. Lee doubtless believed."

"Have a little truth, Professor Cole. Have some indeed, you blubbering butcher—embracer of atrocity, genocidal lunatic, satanic asshole, living, breathing, walking turd."

"Colorful language from a man who clearly doesn't know what's what, who thinks he's on a Christian cruise with lectures by a pagan. An Archer who imagines somehow he could lift a bell-jarred baby off his snapping ribcage. A Hesseltine who clearly needs to be slapped about, have some manners beaten into him and I'm destined, I suppose to do it."

As Cole advanced toward the row where Hesseltine stood and locked with him in a weird tango of toppled, collapsing folding chairs, spinning each other in a head-butting slow-widening circle like a carousel whose propelling batteries had given out.

7.

"I really can't have a situation in which the lecturer I've hired to entertain and enlighten my passengers ends up pummeling them. Surely you can see that. It's intolerable, a term diplomats used to use before declarations of war. Surely you can see that." The Captain spoke slowly, gravely, but softly as if confiding a bit of gossip. He stood at the end of the sparkling green felt long table. Cole sat at the other end, and behind the captain whose blue uniform was starched and pressed perfectly, was a brilliant white LED spot light casting the captain's shadow on the green felt, and depending on the captain's head movements, blinding Cole.

"I wasn't pummeling. How could a man my age pummel anybody?"

"We don't really want to pursue that argument, do we? Take your punishment like the stalwart we imagined you to be. Get off at Nha Trang and fly home in only a very modest disgrace. Failing to lecture effectively on a cruise ship in the South China Sea hardly qualifies for a clothes-tearing session, does it?"

"We?"

"Just me, then. Have it your way."

"It wasn't a pummeling. It was barely a dance between old antagonists. You probably hired him to provide your dwindling audience with some entertainment. Maybe it was a publicity stunt."

"Not the sort of publicity we seek."

"Again, who the hell is 'we'?"

"Just a manner of speech. I am sufficient."

Ducking the light, Cole nodded conceding the Captain's larger, light-blocking role. "How do I fly home from Nha Trang?"

"There is an international airport and we bought your flight ticket originally. It will cost almost nothing to change the departure date and the departure airport. But if that's a concern, you can invoice me for it. The bursar can work that out."

"And my stipend?"

"Stops this day. The bursar can work that out also."

"So this becomes just a vacation disruption."

"Life is so." The captain smiled.

"Yes, when you hold all the power."

"Indeed. All the power," the captain smiled more broadly.

"And what will your passengers, starved for my wisdom about Asia, do for their diversion?"

"Professor Moran will join the crew. It turned out his hesitancy could be solved."

"So pummeling really had nothing to do with this decision."

"Oh it has something. Decisions come from a sudden coherence of elements."

Cole cocked his head to the right and rested his sighing hands sloppily on the table top. "I'm interested in that. Tell me about that."

"Not this trip," the Captain said, turning away.